D0816321

BURN, REMO, BURN!

Chiun stared at the flaming building into which Remo had disappeared. "Hurry, Remo," Chiun said, his face as anxious as a grandmother's.

But Remo didn't come down. The house came down. Eaten by flames, it gave way with a great rending crash, the roof collapsing in a mass of beautiful, terrifying sparks.

The crowd stepped back in stunned horror, giving a low mourning groan. Except one person. Chiun. The master of Sinanju let out a cry like a lost soul.

"Remo!" he wailed. "My son!"

Chiun was wrong. The Destroyer was not dead. But this was no cause for celebration, as Chiun and the world soon learned. What had happened to Remo in that hellish conflagration made death seem sweet—for all of them. . . .

_____ THE DESTROYER #70 _____
THE ELEVENTH HOUR

⊘ SIGNET (0451)

REMO LIVES ON

☐ **REMO: THE FIRST ADVENTURE by Warren Murphy and Richard Sapir** (based on the motion picture written by Christopher Wood). He was the toughest cop in Brooklyn. Until he woke up one morning to see his own name in the obit headlines—and a new face in the mirror. With a new name, a new I.D., and a new job Remo must race against time to save a beautiful Army major—not to mention America—from a death merchant's dream of destruction. . . . (139089—$3.50)

☐ **DESTROYER #67: LOOK INTO MY EYES by Warren Murphy and Richard Sapir.** A malevolent Mindmaster sends Remo and Chiun into battle—but against each other! They are on a collision course—and the world could end not with a bang, but with their crash. . . . (146468—$3.95)

☐ **DESTROYER #68: AN OLD FASHIONED WAR by Warren Murphy and Richard Sapir.** Something strange was happening all over the world. Chiun was the only one who knew what it was . . . but he wasn't telling. With Remo and Chiun divided humanity's ultimate nightmare was coming true by the hands of ancient evil. (147766—$3.95)

☐ **DESTROYER #69: BLOOD TIES by Warren Murphy and Richard Sapir.** Remo and Chiun are sent to stop a deadly assassin only to find out the mysterious hit man was Remo Williams—the one man the Destroyer could not destroy! (148797—$3.95)

Prices slightly higher in Canada.

Buy them at your local bookstore or use this convenient coupon for ordering.

NEW AMERICAN LIBRARY,
P.O. Box 999, Bergenfield, New Jersey 07621

Please send me the books I have checked above. I am enclosing $_____
(please add $1.00 to this order to cover postage and handling). Send check
or money order—no cash or C.O.D.'s. Prices and numbers are subject to change
without notice.

Name_____

Address_____

City_____State_____Zip Code_____
Allow 4-6 weeks for delivery.
This offer is subject to withdrawal without notice.

#70

The Destroyer

THE ELEVENTH HOUR

WARREN MURPHY & RICHARD SAPIR

A SIGNET BOOK

NEW AMERICAN LIBRARY

PUBLISHER'S NOTE

This book is a work of fiction. Names, characters, places, and incidents either are the product of the author's imagination or are used fictitiously, and any resemblance to actual persons, living or dead, events, or locales is entirely coincidental.

NAL BOOKS ARE AVAILABLE AT QUANTITY DISCOUNTS WHEN USED TO PROMOTE PRODUCTS OR SERVICES. FOR INFORMATION PLEASE WRITE TO PREMIUM MARKETING DIVISION, NEW AMERICAN LIBRARY, 1633 BROADWAY, NEW YORK, NEW YORK 10019.

Copyright © 1987 by Richard Sapir and Warren Murphy

All rights reserved

SIGNET TRADEMARK REG. U.S. PAT. OFF. AND FOREIGN COUNTRIES
REGISTERED TRADEMARK—MARCA REGISTRADA
HECHO EN CHICAGO, U.S.A.

SIGNET, SIGNET CLASSIC, MENTOR, ONYX, PLUME, MERIDIAN and NAL BOOKS are published by NAL PENGUIN INC., 1633 Broadway, New York, New York 10019

First Printing, September, 1987

1 2 3 4 5 6 7 8 9

PRINTED IN THE UNITED STATES OF AMERICA

For Bob Randisi, Ric Meyers,
Ted Joy, Ed Hunsburger,
Molly Cochran and Will Murray.

1

Right up until the moment he sold America out, Sammy Kee would have laughed at anyone who called him a traitor to the United States.

Was it treason to love your country so much that you fought to improve it? "And God knows it needs improvement," he would say.

After all, everybody knew that America was a fascist, racist country.

Everybody knew that anyone in jail in America was a political prisoner.

Everybody knew that there was no atrocity committed anywhere in the world so bad that America hadn't committed a worse one.

Everybody knew that there would be peace in the world if only America would stop building nuclear weapons.

Sammy Kee had never been formally schooled in these positions. He had figured them out simply by watching the television network news. Would television lie?

So he repeated all his slogans and he marched against aid to the Nicaraguan contras and he bought every record by Peter, Paul, and Mary and he was still unhappy.

He was unhappy because all three major television networks had refused to hire him as a roving correspondent, even though he had sent each of them, as an audition piece, a fifteen-minute videotape sample which had been his senior project at the UCLA film school and which had earned him the unprecedented mark of A-double-plus.

The tape was a dimly lit, slightly out-of-focus series of interviews with prostitutes, drug dealers, and muggers, all of whom earnestly stated for the camera that Reaganomics had driven them to crime.

The network rejections had left him despondent for two days. Then he decided that the problem wasn't his; it was the problem of the three television networks. First, they weren't ready yet for his hard-hitting brand of independent journalism; and second, they were increasingly under the control of the evil government in Washington, D.C.

Figuring out a way to blame his joblessness on Ronald Reagan instantly made Sammy Kee feel better and it was then that he had his master idea. If the networks would not hire him to prove how bad America was, he would make himself an overseas correspondent and prove how good other countries were. Same church, different door.

And now Sammy Kee had just such a story. All he had to do was to get it home and it would make him the biggest name in television since Geraldo Rivera. Even bigger than Rivera because Sammy had found something more important than empty bottles in Al Capone's old closet.

But first he had to get back to the United States, and he was beginning to think that might not be so easy.

He had tried to reach the airport but the beautiful Asian capital city had been ringed by guards and only an official pass would satisfy them. Kee did not have a pass. All he had was a white cotton blouse and dirty trousers tied at the cuff with ragged blue ribbons in the peasant style. But peasants were not welcome in the capital and they had turned him away without even asking for his nonexistent pass.

So he had ducked under an old vegetable truck waiting at the south-road checkpoint and ridden the axle into the city.

He had not expected the city to be so beautiful. He had been told that it was completely flattened by American bombers thirty-five years ago but it had been rebuilt from the dirt up. It sparkled. There were skyscrapers and massive government buildings, scrubbed as if new, and heroic statues stood in every square. The bland, flat face of the Great Leader stared down from posters and billboards like some sort of benign pancake god.

But the city was also soulless, Sammy Kee discovered after crawling out from under the vegetable truck. Few people walked the streets. Little traffic hummed in the roads. Shops and restaurants were stagnant from lack of trade. Even the neon signs lacked color. And there were the soldiers with the hard boyish faces and almond-shaped eyes that one saw everywhere in this corner of Asia. Only they were more numerous here.

If only he could have slipped past the soldiers, huddled on every corner in their green overcoats and fur caps, Sammy Kee might have found a way out of the country. But two of the soldiers spotted his peasant garb near the Koryo Hotel and shouted to him to stop. Sammy immediately took flight.

He did not know where he ran, only that he took every corner he came upon. The heavy sound of their running boots dogged his path, but Sammy ran faster because they were motivated by duty, but he by fear.

On Turtle Street he saw a familiar emblem on the gate. A flag fluttered on a pole. It was red. And behind the gate, the massive white marble of the Russian embassy sat in the darkness like a sullen ghost.

Sammy ran to the gate. He looked back over his shoulder.

There was no sign of the soldiers. Sammy Kee felt his lunch, some rancid *kimchi* he had found in a garbage can, rise in his esophagus. For the thousandth time he brushed a dirty hand against his trouser leg, feeling the reassuring hard plastic box under the white cotton. What was in that plastic would buy his life, his freedom, and make him a star. If he could get home.

He hesitated before the gate. Then the sound of a military whistle filled the neighborhood. Sammy forced himself to press the buzzer. Only the Russians could protect him, an American in Pyongyang, the capital of the People's Democratic Republic of Korea, where no American had walked free since the Communists took over forty years earlier.

Sammy wiped a tear from his eye as he waited. There was a man in a green uniform coming to the gate. He looked white, which reassured Sammy Kee, even though he himself was not white, but of Korean descent. Sammy had been born in San Francisco.

"What do you want?" the uniformed man said in stiff, formal Korean. He was slight, blondish, like a minor bureaucrat who had been drafted into military service. His most outstanding feature was a pair of horn-rimmed glasses. He was so nondescript that people always remembered the glasses but not the face behind them.

"I want political asylum," Sammy Kee said in English. "I am an American."

The Russian looked as if he had been shot. The

shock of hearing Kee's accent tightened his face. He pressed a hidden switch and unlocked the gate.

"Quickly," the Russian said, and when Sammy Kee hesitated, he yanked the American who looked like a dirty Korean peasant into the compound with such force that Sammy Kee hit the pavement like a tackled halfback.

"Fool," the Russian said, taking Sammy by the arm and lifting him bodily. "If any of my Korean comrades had caught you, I could not have stopped them from having you shot as a spy."

"I want to see the ambassador," said Sammy Kee.

"Later. First, you will answer questions. Who knows you are in this country?"

"No one."

"I mean, what Americans know?"

"No one. I came on my own."

The Russian led Sammy Kee into the basement of the Soviet compound. They went in through a side door obviously used for rubbish disposal. Somewhere a furnace issued a dull roar. The corridor was lined with stone. But the doors were of wood. They looked more substantial than the stone. The Russian pushed Sammy through one of them, locking it behind them.

It was an interrogation room. That was obvious. A simple table sat under a cone of harsh too-white light. The chairs were of uncomfortable wood.

Sammy Kee, surrendering to the situation, sat before he was told to sit.

"I am Colonel Viktor Ditko," the Russian said, and immediately Sammy Kee knew that the man was KGB.

Sammy Kee started to volunteer his name, but the colonel snapped a question first.

"How did you get into this country?"

"By the Yellow Sea. A raft."

"From a submarine?"

"No. I left from South Korea."

"Where did you beach?"

"I don't know. A village."

"How did you get to Pyongyang?"

"By train. From the railhead at Changyon."

The colonel nodded. Changyon was less than one hundred miles south of Pyongyang. Trains ran regularly from Changyon to Pyongyang. Or as regularly as anything ran in North Korea. It was possible for someone with the right racial features and local currency to make such a trip, even if he was an American, so long as he spoke a little Korean and kept to himself.

"You came to North Korea by sea just to turn yourself over to us? You could have applied for asylum in any Western nation. Our embassies are everywhere."

"I didn't come to North Korea to apply for asylum. I'm applying for asylum to get *out* of North Korea. Alive."

"What, then?"

"I came to see Sinanju with my own eyes."

"I have never heard of it."

"It is a place on the West Korea Bay. My grandfather told me of it."

"You are a spy, then," Colonel Ditko said, thinking that Sinanju must be a military installation. "You admit it?"

"No. I am an American journalist."

"That is the same thing," insisted Colonel Ditko. "You have come to this country to spy into the secrets of the military installation at Sinanju."

"No. That isn't it at all. Sinanju isn't a military base. It's a fishing village. The only secret I found there isn't Korean. It's American."

"American?" sputtered Colonel Viktor Ditko. "No American has set foot in North Korea in over forty years—except as a prisoner."

"I have."

"What is the secret?"

"I will tell that to the ambassador when I apply for asylum."

Colonel Viktor Ditko unholstered his pistol and cocked it.

"You will tell me now. I will decide what the ambassador hears, and from whom."

Sammy Kee felt it all drain away at that moment. The hope, the fear, the despair. All of it. He felt numb.

"The proof is in my trousers."

"Bring it out—slowly."

Sammy Kee stood up and shook his tattered cotton trousers. Something bulky slid down one trouser leg and stopped at the cuff. Sammy undid the blue ribbon and, bending to catch what fell out, produced a black plastic box.

The colonel, who had seen many Western films in the privacy of his Moscow apartment thanks to the miracle of video recorders, recognized the object as a video cassette.

He took the cassette eagerly.

"This was recorded where?"

"In Sinanju," Sammy Kee said.

"You will wait," the colonel said, and locked the door behind him to make certain that the order would be obeyed.

Sammy Kee broke down then. He blubbered like a child. It had all gone wrong. Instead of the Soviet ambassador, he had fallen into the hands of a KGB colonel. Instead of bargaining for his freedom, he was a prisoner of an ambitious officer. Probably he would be shot in this very room within the hour.

The KGB colonel was not long in returning. Sammy wiped his eyes on his sleeves and tried to sit up straight. He wanted to crawl under the table instead.

"This is a tape of a fishing village," Colonel Ditko said.

"Sinanju. I told you that."

"Most of this tape is of an old man, sitting on a rock, smoking a pipe, and droning on and on."

"Didn't you listen to what was said?"

"My Korean is not good. I am in this post less than a year."

"Then you don't know."

"No. But you will tell me. Why would an American journalist risk his life and freedom to penetrate North Korea just to tape an old man's life story?"

"It wasn't the old man's life story. It wasn't anyone's life story. It was the story of human civilization. All of the dynasties, and the politics, and the great upheavals in recorded history are a consequence of what has been going on in that little fishing village for five thousand years."

"Are you crazed?"

"Let me start at the beginning."

Colonel Viktor Ditko tossed the cassette onto the plain table with a report like a gunshot. He sat down slowly and folded his wiry arms.

"Start at the beginning, then."

"I was born in San Francisco. My parents were born there too."

"I do not need *your* life story."

"You wish to understand," Sammy Kee said.

"Continue then."

"My grandfather was born in Chongju, here in the north. When I was a boy, he used to sit me on his lap and tell me stories of Korea. Wonderful stories. I can still hear his voice in my head. One of the stories was of the Master of Sinanju."

"A feudal lord?"

"No. You might call the Master of Sinanju a world power of ancient history. He was neither a king nor a prince. But he was responsible for shifting the balance of power among nations countless times throughout recorded history. You might call him history's first superpower."

"What has this fable to do with your being here?"

"Everything. I thought it was a fable too. The Master of Sinanju was an individual of great wisdom and power, according to my grandfather. He was not a single person, but an office. Throughout history there have been many Masters of Sinanju. It was a position handed down from father to son, among a certain family in the village of Sinanju. That family was known as the House of Sinanju, although Sinanju was not the family name."

"It is the name of the village," the colonel said wearily.

"But it was also something else, according to my grandfather. Sinanju was a discipline, or a power, tightly held by the Master of Sinanju and conferred through the family line. Masters of Sinanju used this power to enforce their will, but they never used it to conquer, or to steal. Instead, they hired themselves out to royalty as bodyguards and assassins. Mostly as assassins."

Something stirred in the back of Colonel Viktor Ditko's mind, a half-memory taking shape from the nervous words of this frightened man. A fabulous story of Oriental warriors who possessed superhuman powers. Where had he heard a similar tale?

"What do you mean by power?" he demanded.

"My grandfather claimed that Sinanju was the original martial art. It predates karate, kung fu, and ninjutsu by thousands of years. All later forms of hand-to-hand fighting are copied from Sinanju. But Masters of Sinanju, once they attain what is called the sun source, achieve mental and physical perfection, becoming supernaturally swift and strong. Perhaps invincible. Like gods."

"There are no gods," said Colonel Viktor Ditko, who had learned in school that science was the only legitimate vehicle for realizing mankind's potential.

"The Masters of Sinanju attended the great courts of history," continued Sammy Kee. "They stood beside the pharaohs of old Egypt. They toppled thrones in ancient Rome. They were the secret weapons of the Borgias, and of France's later kings. Whoever hired them, prospered. Any who challenged them, perished. So my grandfather said."

"So?" asked Ditko, trying to isolate the memory. Was it in Tashkent?

"So this. My father claimed that the Masters of Sinanju continued to this day. They hadn't worked as much in this century because of the two world wars, but the current Master of Sinanju still lived in the village, guarding a fabulous treasure and keeping historical records that explained some of the great mysteries of the ages."

"The old man on the tape. He was the Master of Sinanju?"

"No. He was just a caretaker. But let me tell this story as it happened."

"Do so."

"I loved that old tale of my grandfather's, but I never dreamed it had any basis in fact. Until last year. I was in India. I told you I was a journalist. I was covering the chemical disaster there, in Gupta."

"A horrible tragedy. Caused by an American chemical company. Americans can't be trusted with such things."

"I was interviewing a cabinet minister about the tragedy," Kee said. "At first, the minister didn't want to talk to me because I was an American, but when he learned I had Korean parents, he changed his mind. Koreans and Indians had deep historical ties, he told me. I had no idea what he was talking about at the time. I did my story, but nobody bought it and I decided to stay in India."

"A mistake," said Colonel Ditko. He had gone to India once. When he had stepped off the plane, the smell had hit him like a thick hot wall. Even in the modern air terminal, the mixture of chaos and filth was overpowering. He immediately reboarded the Aeroflot jet and returned home, later sending a subordinate to finish the task assigned to him. As punishment, he had been given the worst assignments in the KGB and rotated often. North Korea was only the latest odious post Colonel Viktor Ditko suffered in.

"I became friendly with the minister," Sammy said. "I questioned him about his remark, about the deep ties between India and Korea. It was then he whispered a word I hadn't heard since childhood. The word was Sinanju."

"I see," said Colonel Ditko, who did not see at all.

"The minister told me that India had been one of the greatest clients for the Masters of Sinanju. Sinanju was still highly regarded in their halls of power, even though no Master of Sinanju had worked for an Indian potentate in generations. We compared stories. This man had heard virtually identical stories. He confirmed that the current Master of Sinanju still lived, and had actually visited India only months before. The minister didn't know the details. It was very secret. But the visit somehow involved the United States."

Colonel Viktor Ditko bolted upright in his chair. It creaked.

"Involved. How?"

"I don't know. That didn't interest me so much at the time. But the journalistic possibilities did. Here was a missing piece of history. A secret international power that ran through history like an invisible thread, touching everything, but recorded by no history book. Except the one maintained by the Master of Sinanju. I decided to go to Sinanju."

For the first time, Colonel Ditko nodded in understanding. "You wished to steal the treasure," he said.

"No. For the story. This was one of the great journalistic stories of the century—of any century."

There was that word again, thought Colonel Ditko, "journalistic." It must be some American synonym for "espionage."

"You wanted the secret of Sinanju for yourself."

"No. I wanted to tell the world about Sinanju, its history, its effect on history."

"Tell the world? You had inside information on this great secret and you wanted to tell others?"

"Yes, of course. I am a journalist."

"No, you are a fool. This is very valuable information. If true, the country which employs the Master of Sinanju could be very powerful. But only if this is done in secret."

"Exactly. It *is* being done in secret."

"I do not understand."

"The Master of Sinanju isn't in retirement. He is operating in the modern world, just as his ancestors always have. It's all on the tape. The old man I spoke to told me everything."

Colonel Viktor Ditko felt a chill course up his spine. The room, already cool, seemed colder still. He knew what the Korean-American was leading up to. And the knowledge parched his tongue. He had never been so frightened by something that it dried the juices in his mouth. But at this moment, Colonel Viktor Ditko's tongue sat like a wad of dog hair in his mouth.

"The Master of Sinanju is working for the United States of America," the younger man said.

"This is on the tape?" Ditko demanded.

"Precisely," Sammy Kee said.

"And you want what?" Colonel Ditko asked.

"I want to get back to America. So I can put this story on television."

"Why do you wish to harm your country?"

Sammy Kee looked surprised. "I don't wish to harm my country. I love my country. That's why I want to improve it." He smiled hopefully; surely this sophisticated Russian would understand that.

"You are an idiot," Ditko said. "Why did you not leave the country the way you entered?"

"When I went back to the place where I buried my raft, it wasn't there. I was chased by soldiers but I got away. Now I can't get out of the country. Without an identity card, I can't get food. I haven't eaten in days. I just want to get home and live in peace."

"I see," said Colonel Ditko, who understood that an empty stomach sometimes spoke louder than a man's loyalty.

"Now may I see the ambassador?" Sammy Kee asked.

"You realize that this is not true proof. It is just an old man telling stories. No more credible than your grandfather."

"Sinanju is there. You can see it for yourself. The treasure house is there. I saw it."

"You saw the treasure?"

Sammy shook his head. "No, only the treasure house. It was sealed and I was told that the hand that unsealed it would strangle its own throat if that hand were not of Sinanju."

"And you let an old man's warning stop you?"

"That old man's warning chilled me to my marrow."

Ditko shrugged. "There may be something in what you say. I, too, have heard tales something like what you speak of, in one of our Asian republics. If the Master of Sinanju exists and is an American agent, this could mean much."

"I want to make a deal with the ambassador. Please."

"Idiot! This is too great for an ambassador. If this is what you say, I must deliver this tape to Moscow in person."

"Take me with you, then."

"No. Understand me, American. You live or die at my whim. First, you will transcribe the words contained on your tape. In Korean, and in English."

"I'm never going to see the ambassador, am I?" asked Sammy Kee, who broke into tears again.

"Of course not. Your discovery will be my passport out of this backward country. Perhaps to great rank and responsibility. I will not share it with anyone outside the Politburo."

"What about me?"

"I will decide later. If you set foot outside this room, I will turn you over to the military police. They will shoot you as a spy. Or I may shoot you myself."

"I am an American citizen. These things don't happen to American citizens," Kee said.

"Not in America, young man. But you are in North Korea now and the rules are different."

Ditko left the room and Sammy Kee began to weep. He knew he would never see San Francisco again.

2

His name was Remo and he had returned to Detroit to destroy an American institution.

In any other city in America, arson was not an institution, but a crime. However, in Detroit, since the 1960's, the institution known as Devil's Night had resulted in destruction of property only a little less costly than the firebombing of the German city of Dresden during World War II.

Devil's Night had started as a Halloween prank, when trick-or-treaters had torched a row of warehouses. Because the warehouses were abandoned, no one took the arson seriously. But then it was repeated the next year. And every year after. The torchings grew into a Detroit tradition, and when the city ran out of warehouses and other abandoned buildings in the early 1970's, the tradition spilled over into residential areas. Then people began to worry. By that time it was too late. The animals had been allowed to run free too long. Now Devil's Night was an institution, and no one was safe in Detroit on Halloween night.

This year the city council of Detroit had instituted a dusk-to-dawn curfew. It was an unprecedented move. Curfews, Remo had always thought, were stuff you found in banana republics. Walking down the deserted streets of Detroit, it made him angry that a major American city would be reduced to this, just because of a small lawless minority.

"This is barbaric," Remo said to his companion. Remo was a trim, good-looking man with deep-set dark eyes and high cheekbones. He wore black. Black slacks and a T-shirt. There was nothing unusual about him except for his strangely thick wrists and the fact that he moved like a dark panther. His feet, happening to walk across the windblown pages of a discarded newspaper, did not raise even a crinkle of sound.

"This is America," said Remo's companion. He did not wear black. He wore smoke-gray silk, trimmed with pink, in the form of a kimono. "Barbarism is its natural state. But tonight is very pleasing. I cannot put my finger on it, but it is very pleasant here—for a dirty American city."

"We're the only ones out in the entire freaking city," Remo said.

"We are the only ones who count," said Chiun, the latest in the unbroken line of Masters of Sinanju. His shiny head, adorned with white wisps of hair above each ear, came only to Remo's shoulder. His parchment face was a happy web of wrinkles, dominated by bright eyes. They were a clear hazel, and they made him seem younger than his eighty-plus years.

"This isn't the way it should be, Little Father," Remo said, stopping at a street corner. No traffic moved. There were no pedestrians. Every storefront was dark. In some of them, the dim figures of storeowners waited and watched. Remo saw a shotgun in one man's arm.

"When I was a kid, Halloween wasn't like this."

"No?" squeaked Chiun. "What was it like?"

"Kids walked the streets safely. We went house to house in our trick-or-treat outfits, and every porch was lit. We didn't have to be kept indoors because parents were afraid of razor blades in apples or Valium hidden in chocolate bars. And we didn't set fire to buildings. At worst, we threw rotten eggs at people's windows if they were too stingy to give us candy."

"You were a child extortionist, Remo. Why am I not surprised?"

"Halloween is an American tradition."

"I like silence better," said Chiun. "Let us walk down this street next."

"Why this one?" asked Remo.

"Humor me."

Remo heard the clinking of metal against stone before he had taken three steps.

"This may be them," Remo whispered. "The arsonists Smith sent us to find."

"Were you an arsonist as a child too?"

"No, I was an orphan."

"A fine thing to say to one who has been as your father."

"Cut it out, Chiun. I don't want to spook these guys."

"I will wait here, then. Alone. Like an orphan."

Remo slid up against the brick wall of a tenement building in downtown Detroit. The wall was smudged black from a fire years before. The dead smell of burned things still clung to the building. The sounds were coming from an alley around the corner.

There were three figures kneeling back inside the alley, only dim outlines in the colorless moonlight. To Remo, whose eyes had been trained to gather up and intensify any available light, the scene was as bright as if he had been watching a black-and-white television picture. He watched silently.

"You lose," said one of the youths in a small voice. Remo caught the flash and clink of a penny bouncing off brick.

"What are you guys doing?" Remo asked suddenly, using the same authoritative voice that, in the days when he was a beat patrolman, was as important as his sidearm.

The three teenagers jumped as one.

"Pitching pennies," one of them said. "What's it to you?"

"I didn't know anyone pitched pennies anymore," Remo said in surprise.

"We do."

"I can see that," Remo said. The sight took him back to his childhood, in Newark, New Jersey. He had pitched pennies all over Newark, even though Sister Mary Margaret of Saint Theresa's Orphanage warned him that it was a sinful waste of time as well as pennies which could help feed the poor.

"Don't you guys know there's a curfew on tonight? You could all go to jail."

"Don't make me laugh," the oldest of the three said. "We're underage. They don't send kids to jail."

He had black hair cut in a punk chop and wore a studded collar around his pale throat. The legend "CTHULHU RULES" was written with red Magic Marker across the front of his dungaree jacket. Remo figured Cthulhu must be a new punk rock group.

"Okay. Let me show you how we used to pitch pennies in Newark."

Remo dug into his pocket, producing a few brown coins.

"The object of the game is to pitch the pennies so they bounce as close to the wall as possible, right?" Remo said.

"I usually win," the first youth boasted.

"Watch this." Remo set himself and let fly.

There came a sound like an ice pick being driven through concrete. In the dim light, a black hole appeared in the brick wall.

"Rad!" the three teenagers said at once.

"Too hard," complained Remo. "I'd better lighten up." He fired again.

This time the penny bounced off the wall and knocked over a garbage can. A gray rat ran for its life.

"Hey! Show us how to do that."

"Are you kidding?" Remo said. "I'm not doing it right. Let me try again."

This time Remo's coin hit the wall without a sound, hung flat against the brick for an impossible moment, and slid down to land on its edge, Lincoln's profile flush to the wall.

"Wow!" cried the young man, his face lighting up. "You'll never do that again in a million years!"

"Watch this," said Remo. And he pitched three pennies so fast that they seemed to strike the wall at once. All three landed on their edges, so there were four shiny new pennies in a row.

"Your turn," Remo offered, grinning.

"No way," said the boy. "You win. Teach us to do that."

"If I did that, you'd all be equal, and then what good would playing each other be?"

"We'd play against other kids."

"I'll think about it. But why don't you kids go home?"

"Come on, man. It's Halloween."

"Not in Detroit," Remo said sadly.

"Who are you, mister?"

"The Ghost of Halloween Past," said Remo. "Now shoo."

Reluctantly, the trio shooed.

"Just kids," Remo said as he rejoined Chiun, who

stood with his long-nailed hands tucked into his folded sleeves.

Chiun snorted. "Juvenile gamblers."

"You never pitched pennies as a kid," Remo said. "You wouldn't understand. They sorta remind me of myself when I was young."

"In that we are in agreement," said Chiun, pointing.

Remo followed Chiun's finger with his eyes.

The three penny-pitchers were setting fire to a trashcan in front of a grocery store. They tipped the flaming contents into the doorway.

"Perhaps you could lend them some matches," offered Chiun.

"Damn," said Remo, taking off after them.

The kids scattered when they saw Remo coming. The wooden door of the grocery started to catch. Remo stopped, for a moment uncertain whether to continue to give chase or to stop the fire. He couldn't afford not to do both.

Remo dug out a penny from his pocket, and sighting on the back of the one boy's exploding hairdo, gave it a flip. Remo didn't stop to look at the result. He scooped up the burning trash barrel in both hands, held it lightly but firmly in the pads of his hands so the heat did not burn his fingers. He could do that. It was second nature by now.

Remo capped the burning rubbish with the trashcan, just as an oil-well fire is capped. When he pulled the can away, the pile smoldered, but that was all. He beat the flames from the door with his foot.

There was still a bit of fire at the bottom of the can. Remo squeezed the barrel. It bent in the middle like an aluminum beer can, even though it was corrugated steel, and gave out a screech like a trash compactor. Remo kept squeezing and shaping. The trashcan became a ball. Remo sent it rolling with a kick.

Casually, with the astonished faces of several store proprietors staring at him from behind grimy and steel-gated storefronts, Remo walked up to the youth's prone form.

There was a lump on the back of his head. His face was mushed against the pavement. A bent penny lay beside his cheek.

Remo picked the kid up by the collar of his jacket and slapped his face once, hard. The kid made a *Whahh* sound and asked what happened in a druggy voice.

"There's a new sheriff in town," Remo growled. "I'm it."

"What did you hit me with, a crowbar?"

Remo produced a penny between forefinger and thumb with a bit of sleight of hand. He held the penny up to the boy's widening eyes. The kid had never seen anything so frightening as that penny in his young life. He looked about fifteen.

"Get the picture?" asked Remo.

"Get it away from me! You can't threaten me like this. It's illegal."

"Threaten? Kid, I'm just showing you the joys of numerology."

"Which?"

"Coin collecting."

"That's numismatics. Numerology is about numbers," the boy said.

"In my league, kid, it's both. The coin means your number is up." And Remo touched the penny to the kid's shiny nose. He screamed, even though Remo made only light contact.

"What do you want?"

"Are you part of this Devil's Night thing?"

"This is my first year. Honest. The trashcan was the first time for me."

"I believe you," Remo said. "Anyone who pitches

pennies in the eighties can't be all bad. But if you want a break, you gotta be straight with me."

"Yessir!"

"Good attitude. I want the names of everyone you know who ever set fires on Devil's Night. This year, last year, any year. Anybody you know."

"What for?"

"I'm going to do coin tricks for them. Numismatics, remember?"

"Coin tricks is prestidigitation."

"When I want smart answers, I'll tug on your leash," said Remo.

"Yessir," said the boy, fingering his studded collar. "Only trying to be helpful, sir."

"The names."

"You don't want a whole bunch of names. You want to know one name."

"One name?"

"Yeah. Moe Joakley's. He's the guy behind Devil's Night."

"One guy? Devil's Night has been going for twenty years."

"Moe Joakley. He started it. He keeps it going."

"Why?"

"Who knows? He helps kids to set fires on Halloween. That's all I know. You go up to his place, he gives you a bottle of gas and a book of matches. It's sorta like Halloween, in reverse."

"It's sorta like insanity," said Remo grimly. "This Joakley. Where do I find him?"

"He's on Woodlawn Street." He gave Remo the number.

"Kid, if I let you off with a boot in the pants, will you go home and stay there?"

"Yessir."

"Because if you don't, I'm going to revive another

tradition. Pennies on a dead man's eyes. Only they won't be on your eyes. They'll be *in* your eyes."

The youth had a flash of stumbling home with two copper coins where his wide blue eyes were. Home looked great just then. Maybe he'd be back in time for *Miami Vice*. He didn't walk. He ran.

"I think I straightened that kid out, Little Father," Remo said as he rejoined Chiun.

"Do not speak to me," Chiun said huffily. "You are an orphan. You have no relatives."

"I'm going to call Smith," Remo said, ignoring Chiun's dig. "These arsons have all been the work of one firebug."

"Give my regards to the Emperor Smith and ask him if he has any more inane errands for us to run."

"That's what I want to know too," Remo said, ducking into a smoke-blackened telephone booth.

In the more than a dozen years that Remo had been working for Dr. Harold W. Smith, the two had attempted to work out a workable communications link for when Remo was out in the field. This latest system, Dr. Smith had assured Remo, was utterly foolproof.

Remo had only to punch in a continuous 1. Smith had picked that number because it was the first number and therefore easily remembered. It didn't matter how many times Remo pressed 1. Pressing 1 more than seven times was enough to set the routing sequencer in motion. Before, Smith had told Remo to press 1 a specific number of times. But Remo kept forgetting how many times and Smith had started getting wrong numbers from three-year-olds playing with their home phones. So Smith had made it a continuous 1.

When Remo got Smith on the first try, Remo was amazed. Smith was annoyed. For security purposes, the call was routed through to Divernon, Illinois, microwaved up to a geosynchronous satellite, downlinked to Lubec, Maine, and relayed by fiberoptic cable to an obscure institution in Rye, New York, known as Folcroft Sanitarium, where it rang a secure phone at Smith's desk.

All those switches distorted Remo's voice almost beyond recognition.

"Smitty?"

"Who is this?" demanded Dr. Harold W. Smith in a voice so lemony it could be sold as air freshener.

"Remo."

"You don't sound like Remo," Smith said suspiciously.

"Blame the phone company. It's me."

"Identify yourself, if you are Remo."

"Sure. I'm Remo. Satisfied? Or do you want me to hold a credit card up to the little holes on the receiver?" Remo snarled.

"Okay, it's you," said Smith, who recognized Remo's insubordination, if not his voice. "Is a certain person with you?"

"You mean Chiun?"

"Good. That was a double check. I accept your identification."

"If you're through," Remo said impatiently, "I want to report."

"Have you neutralized the situation in Detroit?"

"Not yet. Listen, Smitty. It's all kids doing this."

"That was our understanding. That's why I instructed you not to kill anyone unless absolutely necessary. Your job is to frighten them off the streets and crush this activity once and for all."

"That could take all night. But there's a better way to go, Smitty. I found out one person is responsible for these fires. An adult. A guy named Moe Joakley."

"What is your source?"

"I caught a little firebug in the act. He told me."

"And you believed him. A teenager?"

"He seemed honest."

"Except for setting fires, is that what you are saying?" Smith said bitterly.

"Look, Smitty. Don't go into a snit too. Chiun is on my case. He's getting tired of this roadshow. You've been sending us hither and yon, catching embezzlers and frightening shoplifters all over America. I thought we were in business to do more than pinch jaywalkers."

"We are," Smith said. "But things are very quiet right now. There hasn't been anything big for you in three months."

"So we're out swatting flies instead of vacationing?"

"This Devil's Night is a big problem, Remo. It's been going on for years, but we've never had you and Chiun available on Halloween Eve before this. This is the perfect opportunity for us to nip this in the bud."

Remo looked out into the night. Fire engines screamed in the distance. They seemed to be everywhere—or trying to be everywhere in Detroit.

"I don't call trying to put out these fires after twenty years of mob rule 'nipping in the bud' exactly," Remo said acidly. "It's going in with defoliants after the forest has burned to the ground."

"Call it what you will. It's your job, Remo. But you may be getting your vacation very soon."

"Are you sure you don't want to send me and Chiun out to patrol the Mexican border for illegal grape pickers after this?"

"Remo," Smith said suddenly. "We may be winning."

"What do you mean 'we'? You're not 'we.' I'm on the front lines while you're sitting on your ass behind your computers pressing keys."

"Remo, the lack of big assignments these past few months may signal the beginning of the end of America's need for CURE. At least, on the domestic front. The Mafia is on the run. Most of the big bosses are behind bars or under indictment. Corporate crimes have been curtailed. Drug use is declining. Crime statistics are down all over. I think the word is finally out: crime doesn't pay."

"Really? You should visit Detroit. It's a city held hostage. And the guy responsible has been getting away with it for a long, long time. His name is Moe Joakley."

"Just a moment," Smith said absently. Remo could hear the busy sound of Smith's fingers at a keyboard.

"Remo. Listen to this: Moe Joakley, thirty-eight years old, born in Detroit, unmarried, former state assemblyman."

"That sounds like the guy."

"If what you've learned is true, we can end Devil's Night tonight."

"Joakley's turned out his last kid firebug," Remo promised. "You can count on it."

"Good. Contact me when your assignment is fulfilled."

"That'll be within the hour. I can't wait to get out of Detroit. It's got some bad memories for me."

Smith, remembering that Remo's last major assignment was in Detroit, said, "I understand." Remo had been assigned to protect Detroit's auto executives from an assassin. For a while, Remo had believed that the assassin was his own lost father. Now Remo knew different, but the experience had reopened a wound that Smith had thought healed over long ago.

"Any luck on the search?" Remo asked.

"I am working on it. I promise you," Smith said. "But it's an immense task. We know nothing about your parents, Remo. Whether they were married. Whether they are dead or alive. There are no records. This is one reason we chose you as our enforcement arm."

" 'Every life casts a shadow,' as Chiun likes to say," Remo told Smith.

"But shadows don't leave tracks."

"That sounds familiar. Who said that?"

"Chiun. In another context."

"He's got an answer for everything," Remo growled, and hung up.

Chiun was still there when Remo left the phone booth. His head was cocked like an inquisitive swallow's, his eyes fixed on some indefinite point in the night sky.

"Little Father, answer me a question. If every life casts a shadow, but shadows don't leave tracks, what is the lesson?"

"The lesson is that words mean what you want them to mean. And do not disturb me, orphan. I am contemplating the rising of the sun."

"Huh?" said Remo. "It's not even midnight."

"Then what is that pink glow beyond yon building?"

Remo looked up. There *was* a pink glow. As he watched, it grew redder, with flickers of orange and yellow shooting through. Smoke boiled up.

"Fire," Remo said. "Come on."

"Are we firemen now?" demanded Chiun. But when he saw that Remo was running without him, Chiun lifted the hem of his kimono and ran like an ostrich.

"You are running with a special grace tonight," Chiun said when he caught up. "Thank you."

"A grace like a fat lady sitting on a cat," Chiun added.

"Save the compliment. Your mind is not on your breathing. I am glad there is no one about to see how the next Master of Sinanju wheezes. Not that I

care what whites think of you. It is important they
do not judge Sinanju by your example, but by mine."

"Blow it out your backside."

And, their pleasantries exchanged, the Master of
Sinanju and his pupil concentrated on their running.
If there had been anyone with a stopwatch on hand,
they would have been clocked at over ninety miles
per hour.

It was a wood frame building. The first floor was
almost completely involved. Fire shot out of every
window. It roared.

On the upper floor, people hung out of the windows. A family. There were three children that Remo
could see. Smoke was pouring out behind them,
forcing them to hang their upper bodies out the
windows just to gulp in breathable air.

"Help us! Help us!" they cried.

A crowd stood helpless on the sidewalk. Remo and
Chiun shoved through them. The heat was intense.
Remo felt the slight film of sweat from his run sud-
denly evaporate.

"I'm going in, Little Father."

"The smoke, Remo," Chiun warned.

"I can handle it," Remo said.

"I doubt that. I am coming with you."

"No. Stay here. We wouldn't be able to carry them
back through that smoke. When I get to the second
floor, I'll throw them down. You catch them."

"Be careful, my son."

Remo put a hand on Chiun's shoulder and looked
down into the old man's young eyes. The bond between them had grown great and the warmth of it
made Remo smile. "I'll see you later, Little Father."
And Remo was gone.

Fire was a bad thing, Chiun knew. But Sinanju
knew how to deal with fire. For what concerned

Chiun was not flames, but the thick billows of smoke ascending into the sky. Smoke robbed the breath, and in Sinanju, the breath was all. It was the focusing point for the sun source that was Sinanju, first and greatest of the martial arts.

Remo ran with his eyes closed. His vision would be useless once he was inside, he knew. Instead he concentrated on charging his lungs with air. He took in the oxygen rhythmically, feeling for his center, attuning himself to the universal forces that enabled him to achieve total harmony within himself. This was Sinanju. That was what Remo had become under Chiun's tutelage.

As he raced for the open, smoke-gorged front door, Remo seemed to see it all unfold before his mind's eyes.

Remo had been a beat cop in Newark. Just a foot-slogging young patrolman with a tour of duty in Vietnam behind him. No one special. In fact, less special than most, because he had no family. His name was Remo Williams, but after a black dope pusher had been found murdered, Remo's badge conveniently beside the body, Remo's name became mud. Remo knew nothing about it. His badge had simply disappeared one night while he slept. The next morning he was being fingerprinted at his own precinct, and none of his fellow cops could meet his eyes.

The trial was swift. Politically, the city wanted to bury this rogue cop who had beaten a black to death. It was a time of great social consciousness, and Remo's rights seemed to be the only ones that didn't matter. Remo could remember his lawyer trying to make a case for insanity by reason of sleepwalking. Remo had refused to lie on the stand. He'd never walked in his sleep in his life.

They sentenced Remo to the electric chair. Just

like that. Remo knew he was innocent. It didn't matter. His friends turned their backs on him. No one visited him on death row. Except for the Capuchin monk in brown robes. The monk had asked Remo a simple question:

"Do you want to save your soul or your ass?"

And he had given Remo a black pill to bite down on just before they strapped him in the chair and clamped the metal helmet, a wire leading out the top, to his shaven head.

Thanks to the pill, Remo was unconscious when they pulled the switch. When he woke up there were electrical burns on his wrists. At first, Remo thought he was dead.

He was assured that he was, but that he shouldn't let it get in his way. The assurance came from the monk in the brown cassock, only now he was in a three-piece suit, a hook sticking out of his left cuff. In the man's good hand there was a photograph of a tombstone. Remo saw his own name cut in the plain granite.

"It's there waiting for you," said the monk, whose name was Conrad MacCleary. "If you say the wrong word."

"What's the right word?" Remo wanted to know.

"Yes."

"Yes, what?"

"Yes, I'm going to work for you," said MacCleary.

And MacCleary had explained it all. Remo had been framed. MacCleary's handiwork. He was proud of it. MacCleary explained that he was ex-CIA, but now he worked for a U.S. government agency that officially did not exist. It was known as CURE. It employed only two people—MacCleary and a Dr. Harold W. Smith, also ex-CIA, not to mention ex-OSS. Smith was ostensibly retired, running a place called Folcroft Sanitarium. Folcroft was CURE'S cover.

Remo had looked around the windowless hospital room.

"This is Folcroft, right?" Remo had asked.

"You got it."

"I don't want it," Remo had said wryly.

MacCleary offered Remo a hand mirror. The face that stared back was not Remo's own. The skin had been pulled tighter, emphasizing the cheekbones. His hairline had been raised by electrolysis. The eyes were more deeply set, and hinted of the East. The mouth thin, almost cruel, especially when Remo smiled. He was not smiling then. He didn't like his new face.

"Plastic surgery," MacCleary explained.

"What'd they use? Silly Putty? I don't like it."

"Your opinion doesn't enter into it. You no longer exist. The perfect agent for an agency that doesn't exist."

"Why me?" Remo asked, working his stiff facial muscles.

"I told you. You're perfect. No family. No close friends. No one to miss you, Remo."

"A lot of people fit that profile," Remo said flatly, sitting up in bed.

"Not many of them with your skills. I did field work in Vietnam. I saw you in action once. You were good. With a little work, you'll be good again."

Remo grunted.

"You're also a patriot, Remo. It's in your psychological profile. Not many people feel about America as you do. You're getting a raw deal, but let me explain it in terms you can appreciate."

Remo noticed that a break in his nose had been repaired. One improvement, anyway.

"A few years ago a young energetic President assumed office and discovered America was dying slowly from a rot too deep to fix with new laws or legislation. The Mafia had its tentacles in corporate America. Drugs had infiltrated all levels of society. Judges were corrupt, lawmakers for sale. There was no solution, short of declaring permanent martial law. Believe me, it was considered. But it would have meant admitting that the great Democratic experiment did not work. The Constitution was about to turn into so much cheap paper.

"But this President saw a way out. He created CURE, the ultimate solution to America's decay. The President knew he could not fight lawlessness legally. It was too late for that. So he came up with a way to protect the Constitution by breaking it. CURE. Empowered to secretly fight America's internal problems. At first, it was Smith and me. It seemed to work. But crime continued to grow. Things got worse. And the President who had given CURE a five-year mandate was assassinated."

Remo remembered that President. He had liked him.

"The next President extended CURE'S mandate indefinitely," MacCleary continued. "And gave us a new directive: CURE was sanctioned to kill. But only one man could be that enforcement arm. More than one would have turned America into a secret-police state. It requires a professional assassin. You, Remo."

"That's crazy. One man can't solve everything. Especially me."

"Not as you are now. But with the right training."

"What kind of training?"

"Sinanju."

"Never heard of it."

"That's the beauty of it. No one knows it exists. But it's going to turn you into America's indestructible, unstoppable, nearly invisible killing machine. If you accept."

Remo looked at his new face in the mirror and then at the photograph of his grave.

"Do I have a choice?"

"Yes. But we'd rather you do it for America."

And Remo had accepted. That was almost two decades ago. MacCleary had died. Remo later met Smith, and most important, Chiun, who had dodged a revolver of bullets Remo had fired at him as a test and then threw Remo to the floor like a child. Chiun had taught him Sinanju, at first reluctantly, then with passion.

And Remo was using Sinanju now, racing into the roaring flames with his eyes squeezed shut, trusting in his training, trusting in the sun source.

Eyes closed, Remo avoided the fire easily. His ears picked out the pockets of roaring flames. He moved away from them. Where he couldn't avoid them, he ran through them. But ran so fast the licking tongues had no chance to ignite his clothes. Remo could feel the short hairs on his exposed arms grow warm. But they did not ignite either.

Remo found the stairs leading up to the second floor by sensing the furious updraft. His acute hearing told him there were no people on the first floor. There were no racing heartbeats of panic, no smell of fear-induced sweat, no sounds of movement. And most important, no smell of burning flesh.

Remo went up the stairs, his lungs pent. He released a tiny breath with each floating step. He dared not release too much at one time because he dared not inhale. The greedy flames ate all the oxygen. His lungs were left with just smoke and floating ash.

It was just as bad on the second floor. Remo dropped to his stomach, where the rising smoke did not boil, and quickly peered around. A long corridor with rooms going off on both sides.

And the sounds of panic. Remo ran to them. He

encountered a locked door, locked to keep the smoke and fire out. Remo popped the door from its hinges with an open-handed smack. The door fell inward like a wooden welcome mat.

Remo opened his eyes again. They were here. The whole family. They were hanging out the windows and didn't see him.

"Hey!" Remo yelled, going toward them. "I'm here to help."

"Thank goodness," the young wife said.

"Save the children first," called the husband, trying to see Remo through the eye-smarting smoke. He was holding a two-year-old boy out the window with both hands.

"Chiun?" Remo called down.

"I am here," said Chiun, looking up. "Are you well?"

"Yeah, Here, catch this kid," Remo said, snatching the boy from his father's arms and tossing him to Chiun.

"My baby!" the mother screeched. But when she saw the miracle of a seemingly frail old Oriental catching her tiny son in his arms and offering him up for inspection, she was relieved.

"The girl next," said Remo.

And Remo lowered a girl in pigtails, dropping her into Chiun's upraised arms.

"You're next," Remo told the mother.

"Thank God. Who are you?" the mother sobbed.

"I'm going to lower you as far as possible," Remo said, ignoring the question, "then drop you. Okay?" The flames had crept down the hallway, eating the wallpaper like a voracious animal, and were licking at the doorjamb. "Don't worry."

Remo hoisted the woman out by her arms. Chiun caught her easily, lightly.

"Now you," Remo told the father.

"I'll jump, thanks." And he jumped. Chiun caught him too.

Remo stuck his head out the window.

"That's everyone?"

"You forgot Dudley," the girl in pigtails cried. Tears were cutting rivers down her soot-streaked cheeks.

"Right. Hang on."

"Wait!" the father called up. But Remo didn't hear him.

Remo recharged his lungs, but the smoke had already touched them. His eyes were tearing. He shut them.

In the corridor, Remo danced past the flames, focusing beyond their angry crackle and snap, listening for a sound. Any sound. He zeroed in on a tiny, racing heartbeat. Remo followed the sound to the end of the corridor, where the smoke was thick. He pushed past a half-open door. The sound was low. On the floor.

Remo hit the floor and crawled. He knew that children instinctively hid under or behind furniture when frightened. He felt a dresser, but it was flush to the wall. He knocked over a chair. Then he found a small bed. A child's bed. The heartbeat was coming from under it.

Remo reached in, touched something warm. He grabbed it. It was small and warm and struggled like a newborn, and Remo ran with it. He found a window, shattered the glass to harmless powder with a fast tattoo of his fingers that upset its crystalline structure on the molecular level.

Remo stuck his head out the window. He smelled air. He sucked it in gratefully. Then he looked in his hand. He saw a brown-and-white tabby cat.

"Damn," Remo said. And he tossed the cat, which landed safely in the backyard and scampered off.

Remo went back into the smoke and flames. But he heard nothing.

"Hey! Anyone here? Anyone!" he cried. He had visions of a child, maybe a baby in a bassinet, over-come by smoke and not breathing.

Remo went through the rooms of the upper floor like a frantic tornado. He used his hands and his ears. His eyes were useless, but in his concern he opened them anyway, seeking, searching. And found nothing.

Finally, the flames were too much. He found himself cut off from the stairs. He couldn't get to a window, either.

Remo jumped from a standing start and tore holes in the plaster ceiling. He pulled himself up, and got to the flat roof.

There, Remo took in a recharging breath. Half of it was smoke. He coughed. Tears streamed from his eyes, but not all of them were from the smoke.

The roof was hot. Remo got to the front side. He could see the upturned faces below. A larger crowd was there. Fire engines pulled up. Hoses were being dragged out and attached to fire hydrants by yellow-slickered firemen.

"I couldn't find him," Remo cried. "Just a cat."

"That's Dudley!" the girl in the pigtails yelled back.

"We tried to tell you," the father called up. "I'm sorry."

But Remo didn't feel sorry. He felt immense relief.

"I'm coming down," he said.

"Hurry, Remo," said Chiun, his face anxious as a grandmother's.

But Remo didn't come down. The house came down. Eaten by flames to its very shore timbers, it gave way with a great rending creak of wood and seemed to snuff out the fires in the first floor. The roof collapsed in a mass of beautiful sparks and Remo was lost from sight.

The crowd stepped back in stunned horror. They were too shocked to speak or react. Only when the smoke suddenly surged up again to obliterate all the pretty sparks did they react.

The crowd gave a low mourning groan. Except one person. Chiun. The Master of Sinanju let out a cry like a lost soul.

"Remo!" he wailed. "My son!"

Only the spiteful snap of consuming fire answered him.

3

Chiun, reigning Master of Sinanju, last of the line of
Masters of Sinanju, trainer of the white American
Remo in the art of Sinanju, saw the five-thousand-
year history of his art disappear into a boiling mass
of crashing timbers and the horror of it shocked him
to his very soul.

But only for mere seconds. Chiun bounded into
the ruins.

There was no longer a door as such. Just a twisted
frame that had been a doorjamb. Chiun went through
it, eyes closed, breath held deep within his lungs,
willing his body temperature to rise. It was the way
of Sinanju when dealing with fire.

The implosion seemed to have knocked out the
inferno. Wood burned and smoldered, but not as
before. Soon, Chiun knew, oxygen would recirculate
back into the ruins and what now smoldered would
soon again burn. And burn furiously. The half-
collapsed house would become an inferno once more.

Chiun had only minutes.

"Remo!" he called.

When there came no answer, the Master of Sinanju
knew fear.

Chiun knew that there were stairs near him. He had heard Remo's soft footsteps climb them but minutes before. Chiun went up those stairs, but he found the way blocked.

The Master of Sinanju dug into fallen timber and plaster, clearing the way. If Remo had been a tornado when he had moved through the second floor, Chiun was a typhoon, mighty, raging, implacable.

"Remo!" he called again. Then, in an anguished voice, "My son! My son!"

Chiun found Remo entangled in a pile of burning supports. Remo hung, head down, like a discarded puppet in a junkyard. His eyes were closed in his ash-smeared face. Flames were eating his ragged T-shirt. And worst of all, his head hung at a peculiar angle, his throat pinned between two blackened joists.

"Remo," Chiun said faintly, a deep cold took his mighty heart.

The Master of Sinanju attacked the pile swiftly. He slashed Remo's burning shirt from his body with quick swipes of his long nails. Throwing it away, he next separated the wood that clamped Remo's neck, catching Remo's head tenderly in his hands.

Chiun saw that Remo's throat was discolored. Blue. Almost black. He had never seen such a bruise before and feared that his pupil's neck had been broken. His deft caress of Remo's neck vertebrae told him it was not so.

"Remo? Can you hear me?"

Remo did not hear the Master of Sinanju. Chiun placed a delicate ear to Remo's bare chest. There was a heartbeat, faint at first, then growing stronger. But Chiun did not recognize the rhythm. It was not Sinanju rhythm. It did not even sound like Remo's heartbeat, a sound Chiun knew well. He often lay awake at night listening to it, knowing that as long as it beat, the future of Sinanju was assured.

"What strangeness is this?" Chiun whispered to himself, gathering Remo up in his arms.

Chiun had not taken Remo three paces when Remo came to life with a violence.

"It is all right," said Chiun gently, "It is Chiun. I will carry you to safety, my son."

But the eyes that looked up at his were strange. They were dark, like Remo's eyes, but they held a strange red light. As they focused on Chiun's face, the features came alive. And the expression was terrible, un-Remo-like.

And the voice that emerged from Remo's bruised bluish throat was more terrible still.

"Who dares profane my body with his touch?"

"Remo?"

Remo pushed Chiun, and the force was so great that Chiun was not prepared for it. Chiun fell backward.

"Remo! Have you gone mad?" said Chiun, picking himself off the floor.

And the next words that emerged from Remo's mouth told the Master of Sinanju that his pupil was not mad.

"Where is this place? Am I in Hell of Hells? Kali! Show yourself! The Lord of the Lightnings challenges you to battle. I am at last awakened from my long slumber."

"You have no enemies here," Chiun said firmly, almost reverently.

"Be gone, old man. I have no truck with mortals."

"I am Chiun, Master of Sinanju."

"I am created Shiva, the Destroyer; Death, the shatterer of worlds."

"And?"

"Is that not enough?"

"There is more. 'The dead night tiger made whole by the Master of Sinanju,' " Chiun recited. "Do you not remember?"

"I remember nothing of you, old man. Be gone, before I slay you like the insect that you are."

"Remo! How could you—" But Chiun cut off his own words. He knew he was no longer speaking to Remo Williams. But the avatar of something greater. And he bowed.

"Forgive me, O Supreme Lord. I understand your confusion. All will be explained to you. Allow this humble servant to guide you from this place of turmoil."

"I need no guide," said the voice from Remo Williams, and he fixed such a gaze on the Master of Sinanju that Chiun felt his heart quail.

"The flames will return soon, Supreme Lord," Chiun insisted. "You do not wish to be in this place when they do."

But Remo ignored him, casting his imperious eyes over the wreckage of flame and ruin. Smoky shadows played over his bare chest. Remo's body was bathed in a scarlet glow. It made him look satanic.

Chiun felt his own breathing weaken. He could not stay in this place much longer. Sinanju breathing techniques worked only where one could breathe. Soon, that would be impossible.

A crafty look wrinkled his visage.

Chiun sagged to the floor.

"Oooh. I am dying," he said, lying on his face. "I am an old man, and the breath is leaving my poor body."

When he heard no reaction, Chiun lifted his head and stole a peek at Remo. Remo was standing by a window, staring out in the night sky, his face troubled.

"I said, I am dying," Chiun repeated. Then he groaned.

"Then die quietly," said Remo.

"Remo!" Chiun squeaked, shocked. And he knew Remo was beyond his reach.

Chiun found his feet as the flames kicked up again. The smoke, which had hung like a thin film in the air, now began to boil anew with the return of air circulation. The dull furnace sound under his feet told Chiun that the only escape now would be through the window.

While Chiun was agonizing over having to leave Remo to the flames, glass shattered in one of the rooms. Then, in another. Chiun could hear the water. Fire hoses were being played on the house, breaking the windows all along the front. The smash of glass came from the next room.

Chiun waited.

Like a gale, a torrent of water came through the window where Remo stood. Remo was pushed back by the sheer force of thousands of gallons of water forced through a high-pressure hose.

Chiun did not hesitate. He scooped up Remo in his arms, and Remo did not resist. He was stunned. Chiun silently thanked his ancestors.

Chiun carried Remo to a rear wall, where the fire damage was less. At the end of the corridor, there was a blank wall. Holding Remo in his arms, he kicked at the wall, in the corners, where he sensed they were most vulnerable.

The wall bulged outward. Chiun gave a square kick to the center of the wall. The wall fell out like a soggy graham cracker.

Chiun vaulted to the soft grass of the backyard, his kimono belling like a gentle parachute, but it was the old man's spindly legs which cushioned the impact for them both.

Gently Chiun laid Remo on the clipped grass.

He stepped back respectfully and folded his arms within the sleeves of his kimono. He did not know which he expected, gratitude or wrath, but he was prepared to face either. He was the Master of Sinanju.

Remo's eyes fluttered open. They did not focus at first. But when they did, they focused on Chiun.

"You saved me," Remo said slowly.

"I did, Supreme Lord."

"Supreme *what?*" Remo demanded, sitting up. "Is that some kind of Sinanju insult? Like 'pale piece of pig's ear'?"

Chiun stepped back as if struck a blow.

"Remo? Is that you?"

"No, it's Lon Chaney, Jr. I just look like Remo because I'm going to play him in a movie. What's with you?"

"Oh, Remo. My ancestors smile upon us. You have no ill effects?"

"My throat feels sore."

"Smoke," Chiun said, touching his own throat. "It will pass. I inhaled some too."

And then Chiun groaned and clutched at his heart and fell over like a sapling bending to an insistent wind.

"Little Father? Are you okay?" Remo demanded.

Chiun lay in the grass unmoving. His breathing was shallow. Remo started applying mouth-to-mouth resuscitation. He was still doing it when a pair of firefighters came around the corner with hoses.

"How is he?" one of the firemen asked.

"I don't know," Remo said distractedly. "He's breathing. But he's not responding. Get some oxygen. Hurry!"

They yelled for oxygen and the paramedics in their orange vests came with a portable tank. Remo knocked them aside and placed the clear plastic mask against Chiun's face.

"Nobody touches him except me," Remo said savagely.

"Take it easy, Mac. We're here to help."

The family Remo had saved came up too.

"That's the man who rescued us," the father said. "The one who was inside when the house fell. Are you all right, mister?"

"Yeah," Remo said. "But Chiun isn't. I don't know what's wrong with him. He got me out okay. He can't be hurt. Chiun! Please wake up."

The paramedic offered an opinion. "He doesn't seem to be burned, or in shock. Must be smoke inhalation. We'd better get him to the hospital."

"Hospital?" Remo said dazedly.

"Yeah," said the paramedic. "Please step aside while we load him on the gurney."

"Load him, my ass," Remo snapped. "He's not a sack of potatoes. I'll do it."

"That's our job. You're not qualified."

When Remo turned, the look in his eyes made the paramedic reconsider. Suddenly.

"On second thought, how qualified do you have to be to lift an old guy onto a gurney? Let me hold it straight for you, buddy."

Gently Remo lifted Chiun onto the wheeled gurney, arranging the hem of his kimono so that it modestly covered his pipestem legs. Chiun was always modest about his body, Remo thought to himself, and if he woke up suddenly, with legs bared to the world, there would be hell to pay.

They wheeled Chiun into the ambulance and Remo climbed in.

Just before the doors shut, the little girl with the pigtails came up, with her cat in hand.

"Thank you for saving Dudley, mister," she said.

"Don't mention it, kid," Remo said hoarsely. His mind was numb. All through the ride to the hospital he held the oxygen mask to Chiun's expressionless face and tried to remember which gods Masters of Sinanju prayed to, and what the correct words were.

*　　*　　*

In the emergency room, there was a minor delay when the admissions-desk clerk wanted Remo to fill out insurance forms for Chiun.

"He doesn't have insurance," Remo told the attendant. "He's never been sick in his entire life."

"I'm sorry. We can't admit this man. But the Deaconess Hospital has a charity ward. It's only twenty minutes away."

"He's sick!" Remo said. "He may be dying."

"Please lower your voice, sir. And be reasonable. This is a very prestigious institution. We have only the finest doctors from the finest medical schools. You can't expect them to treat just *any* patient. Especially those who can't pay their bills. The doctors have a right to earn a living."

And then Remo showed the admitting attendant that there were other rights. Like the right to life, liberty, and the pursuit of happiness.

He drove the point home when he drove the man's retractable pen through the palm of his hand.

"Sign him in," Remo growled.

"I can't!"

"Why not?"

"That's my only pen."

"Where do you fill in the name?"

The attendant pointed with the finger of his undamaged hand.

In that space Remo wrote Chiun's name, guiding the man's wrist so that the pen embedded in his palm scrawled the name in the proper space, in a mixture of ink and blood.

"Thank you," moaned the attendant, as Remo pushed the gurney onto an elevator.

Dr. Henrietta Gale was adamant.

"I'm sorry. Not even relatives are allowed in the

examination room. And it's obvious that you couldn't possibly be related to this Oriental gentleman."

"I'm coming in." And to make his point, Remo adjusted Dr. Gale's dangling stethoscope. He adjusted it so that it clutched at her throat like a too-tight choker.

"Those are hospital rules," she said in a Donald Duck voice.

"I can make it tighter," Remo warned.

"Loosen it just a smidge," Dr. Gale gasped, "and you can come in."

Remo wrenched the twisted metal free.

"Thank you," Dr. Gale said formally. "Now, if you'll follow me."

They had Chiun in a hospital bed. An I.V. ran from one exposed arm. He was hooked up to a battery of machines, most of which Remo didn't recognize. An electrocardiogram registered his heartbeat as a blue blip on a screen. Oxygen was being administered through breathing tubes inserted in his nose.

An orderly cut Chiun's kimono free of his chest, making Remo wince. It was a good thing Chiun wasn't awake to see that.

Dr. Gale examined Chiun's eyes with a penlight.

"No contraction of the pupils," she mused. "Wait a minute. There they go."

"What's that mean?" Remo asked.

"Please stay out of our way, sir. We are working. It means that his eyes were not registering the light, but suddenly they are now.

"That's good, isn't it?"

"I don't know. I've never seen such delayed reflexes."

"Oh."

"Nurse?" Dr. Gale called to a blond in white.

"Heartbeat down, B.P. one-twenty over forty. Breathing shallow but regular."

"He's very old," Dr. Gale said to no one in particular.

"Can you help him?" Remo said anxiously.

"He's not responding to the oxygen. This could be more than just smoke inhalation. I'm not sure what. We're going to run some tests."

"Anything," Remo pleaded. "Just help him."

"All right, whoever you are. But I suggest you sit down and stop pacing the floor like an expectant father. We're going to be quite busy for the next few hours."

"You got it. I'm going to make a phone call."

"Just as long as you do it out in the corridor."

"Smitty?" Remo asked when he got Folcroft on the line.

"Give me the code for successful completion," Smith said dryly.

"Screw the code. I'm at the hospital."

"You were supposed to eliminate your target, not hospitalize him," Smith said.

"Forget him. This is more serious. Chiun has just been admitted. He's sick."

"Oh no," said Smith. He paused, "This is another one of his schemes to extort more gold for his village, isn't it? We just negotiated another contract. The submarine is about to leave for his village. No," Smith corrected, "tell Chiun that the sub has *already* left with the gold. It's too late to renegotiate."

"Will you forget your budget and listen to what I'm saying? Chiun is really sick. This is serious. The doctors can't figure out what's wrong with him."

"Come, come, Remo. Chiun is a Master of Sinanju. One of the most powerful creatures to ever walk upright. He can't be sick. Masters of Sinanju never get sick—do they?"

"They die, Smith. You know that. They don't live forever."

"You have a point," said Smith, his voice mixing worry and doubt. "But this had better not be malingering on your part. I don't want you thinking that because we now see the light at the end of the tunnel for CURE that you can start slacking off."

"Smitty, it's a good thing you're not standing in front of me right now," Remo said softly.

Smith cleared his throat. "Perhaps you had better fill me in on Chiun's medical status."

"I got caught in a fire. The house collapsed. I don't remember anything that happened after that. The next I knew I was on the ground and Chiun was standing over me. I think he carried me out while I was unconcious. Then he just fainted or something. One minute he was talking some nonsense, the next he was out cold. They're running tests on him now."

"When does the doctor expect results?"

"I don't know. Sounds like they'll be half the night. I'm worried."

"So am I, Remo. But I'm getting news reports of numerous fires raging all over greater Detroit."

"Forget the firebugs. We'll get them next year. I'm staying with Chiun."

"Let me remind you, Remo, that your investigation has turned up the name of the single motivating person behind Devil's Night. And that person, directly or indirectly, is responsible for the fire that caused this accident."

"Joakley isn't going anywhere."

"If you don't want to get him for me, or for CURE, or for America, then get him for Chiun. He's the reason Chiun's been hurt."

Remo's eyes narrowed. "Yeah. Chiun would want me to do that. Smitty, I'll get back to you."

*   *   *

The headlines the next morning read: "RUNAWAY ROBOT MURDERS EX-DETROIT ASSEMBLYMAN."

The short item was accompanied by a photograph of the victim—a smiling broad-faced man. The caption gave his name as Moe Joakley. There was also a police sketch of the suspect. The suspect was eight feet tall and had six arms. One of the arms ended in a giant ball-peen hammer, another in a hydraulic vise, and the rest in various other implements of destruction, including a flamethrower. The suspect's body consisted of stainless-steel jointed sections, like a centipede's body. It looked like a cross between an industrial robot and a Hindu statue.

The article admitted that the sketch was fanciful, but the police artist insisted that the damage done to the late Moe Joakley could only have been inflicted by a phantasm such as he drew.

Moe Joakley would have disagreed. He had been staring out the plate-glass window of his den, binoculars in hand, at precisely the stroke of midnight. His police scanner roved the band, stopping at every emergency call. To the south, fires burned out of control. A row of apartment houses smoldered on the east side. That was good. It was overdue for urban renewal.

It had been more than two hours since the last of the trick-or-treaters knocked on Moe Joakley's door looking for the kind of treat only he supplied in the whole city. Usually the last of them showed up before ten o'clock. But the fires often burned till two. Not a bad number this year. But only four deaths. Up one from last year, but down from the all-time high of fifty-five in 1977. Those were the good days.

Moe Joakley poured himself a drink. Halloween night. It was his favorite time of year. For better than twenty years, Moe Joakley had ruled Detroit on

Halloween—an invisible king enthroned in a glass tower.

Moe Joakley hadn't always been king. Once, he had been a teenager who just liked to set fires. Back in the sixties, there had been an exodus of people and businesses. Detroit, racked by crime and poverty, was turning into a ghost town. No one cared. And because no one cared, Moe Joakley had set fire to a row of warehouses one Halloween night while in the throes of his very first peach-wine drunk.

It felt good. When he sobered up, Joakley knew he couldn't do that sort of thing every day. It was special. So he counted the days and nights until the next Halloween. And set fire to another group of buildings.

The third year, he got together a gang. That's when it really started. The press called it Devil's Night. Moe Joakley was proud of that.

As the years went by, some of Joakley's teenage fellow arsonists grew up and dropped out of the annual ritual. That upset Moe Joakley. Friends shouldn't turn their backs on other friends. The first friend to do that was Harry Charlot. He had gotten married. A dumb excuse, Moe Joakley thought at the time.

So he had set fire to Harry's house that very next Halloween. Harry died. His wife too. It was the first time Moe Joakley had tasted blood. He liked it.

But he was also smart enough to know that an adult couldn't continue to get away with the same pranks teenagers did forever. One year, he stopped, too. Not stopped causing fires, just setting them personally. Moe had a reputation to live up to. He had gone into politics, and succeeded in getting himself elected assemblyman of his home district. He was swept into office on a platform of stopping Devil's Night.

And sure enough, the next year, the fires in his district stopped. They went up in all other districts. That was thanks to the teenagers Joakley had sent out.

Joakley knew that wisdom was passed from older kids to younger. Once he had started one group setting fires, it was inevitable that younger brothers and sidekicks would be drawn into Devil's Night. And there were always new kids coming up every year.

Twenty years, and no one ever turned Moe Joakley in.

So he sat enjoying the pretty red flames in the distance, not noticing the grandfather clock toll the final midnight of his misspent life.

He didn't expect a knock on the door this late. But Moe went to the door anyway.

"Who is it, please?"

"Trick or treat!" an unfamiliar voice said. It sounded adult.

"Who is it?"

"Is this Moe Joakley?"

"That's the name on the brass plate. But it's after midnight. Go away. I'm out of candy."

"I don't want candy."

"Then what?"

"You know."

"Tell me," Moe Joakley prompted.

"I want to burn something."

Moe Joakley hesitated. Out his window, the fires were dying down. What the hell? Maybe this could go on all night. He opened the door.

The man at the door was in a funny costume. His chest was bare, and there was a deep bruise around his throat. Must be a new fad, Joakley thought to himself. The punk look must be dead.

"Come on in. You're older than most of the others."

"You the guy that hands out the firebug stuff?" Remo Williams asked coolly.

"Shhh!" said Moe Joakley. "Here, take a bottle."

"I'm not thirsty," said Remo.

"It's not to drink. It's full of gasoline."

"Oh," said Remo.

"If the cops catch you, offer them the bottle. Usually they'll let you go and keep it, thinking it's booze."

"What if they open it first?"

"Then you're on your own. If they question me, I'll do two things. First, I'll admit giving you the bottle, but I'll say you drank the booze and then filled it with gasoline yourself."

"And the second?" Remo inquired politely.

"I'll burn your house down and everyone in it."

"Nice guy."

"Hey, you want to play, you gotta pay. Be on your way now."

"Wait a minute. Don't you want to tell me which buildings I should torch?

"Be creative. Just don't touch the four blocks around this one. These people pay for protection. And no auto companies. They pay for protection too."

"You do this for the money?" Remo said.

"What else? Money. And I like to see things burn."

"I'll try not to disappoint you," Remo said. He twisted off the sealed cap and gasoline fumes rose into the room like a chemical genie. "Gasoline, all right," Remo said.

"High octane. Only the best. Now be off."

"Got any matches?"

"Oh, sure." Joakley dug into the pocket of his purple dressing gown. "Here you are."

Remo reached for the book and accidentally spilled half the bottle over Moe Joakley's ample tummy.

"Watch it! This is pure silk!"

"Sorry," said Remo. "Here, let me help you wipe it off."

"What are you doing? You can't wipe this stuff off with your bare hands."

Moe tried to back away but Remo's hands held him. They were rubbing at the front of his dressing gown so fast they blurred. The gown began to feel strangely warm. A curl of smoke drifted up.

"Hey!" Joakley said again. And then went up in flames with a loud *Whooosh!*

"Arrgh!" Moe Joakley screamed. "I'm on fire!"

"Does it hurt?" Remo asked solicitously.

"Arrgh!" Joakley said again. Remo took that as a yes.

"Now you know how it feels," Remo said. "The only person who ever cared for me is in a hospital because of you."

"I'm burning. I'm burning to death. You can't let me burn."

"Wanna bet?"

A smell like roast pork filled the room as Moe Joakley scurried around the room like a flaming pinwheel. And Remo knew that, whatever he did, he couldn't just let Moe Joakley burn. Burning was too easy.

"Get down on the floor," Remo yelled. "Roll on the rug."

Moe Joakley rolled on the rug like a dog rolling in something that stank, only he rolled faster. The gas-fed flames refused to die. In fact, they got worse because the rug caught.

Remo grabbed a heavy blanket from the bedroom and threw it over Moe Joakley's squirming, flaming body, trying to smother the fire.

Joakley screamed louder.

Remo suddenly remembered reading somewhere that flames could be extinguished by slapping them hard. He began slapping Moe Joakley's body through the blanket. The screams suddenly stopped and little tendrils of smoke curled up from under the blanket.

"Is it out?" Remo asked.

"I dunno. I still feel hot."

Remo kept slapping the man. Harder now. The smacking sounds grew louder. So did the screams.

"I think you can stop now," Joakley howled.

But Remo didn't stop. He kept slapping at the wriggling form under the blanket. His hands drummed like pistons. The sounds emerging from under the blanket grew meatier—occasionally punctuated by a mushy crushing of bone.

Moe Joakley's protests grew mushy too, like the burbling of a baby.

Gradually, under Remo's drumming hands, the shape under the blanket lost its human outlines.

When Remo was done, the blanket was almost flat. He stood up and left the apartment in silence. He did not look under the blanket. He did not need to.

The next day, after the body was discovered by a maid, the police looked under the blanket. Their first thought was that they had discovered an alien life form.

"Looks like an amoeba," suggested the medical examiner. "Or maybe a dead fetus."

"Too big for an amoeba," said a detective.

"Or a fetus."

When the medical examiner found a human tooth lying on the rug, he realized for the first time the hairless thing under the blanket had once been a man. He got violently sick. Then he went into another line of work.

They got two morgue attendants to load Moe

Joakley's roasted carcass into a body bag. They had to use shovels, and Joakley kept slipping off like a runny omelet.

The morgue attendants went into new lines of work too.

And although a thorough investigation was conducted, no trace of the runaway robot murder suspect was ever discovered.

4

"Mr. Murray. He's asking for you."

In the waiting room of the hospital, Remo Williams did not look up. He wore fresh clothes that he had picked up at his hotel, where he had quickly showered the soot from his body. A turtleneck jersey helped conceal the livid bruise on his throat.

"Mr. Murray," the nurse said again, tapping him gently. "You are Remo Murray, aren't you?"

"Oh, right, yeah, Remo Murray," Remo said. It was the cover name under which he'd registered at the Detroit Plaza Hotel. He had forgotten it.

"How is he?" Remo asked, following the nurse into the ward.

"He's comfortable," she said noncommittally.

Dr. Henrietta Gale was hovering at Chiun's bedside. She frowned when she saw Remo enter.

"Normally, I would not allow this, but poor Mr. Chiun insists."

Remo ignored her. "Little Father, how do you feel?" he asked gently.

"I am hurt," Chiun said, staring at the ceiling.

"How bad?"

"To my very core," Chiun said, refusing to meet

Remo's eyes. "I am told while I lie between life and death you deserted my bedside."

Remo bent to Chiun's ear. "The hit, remember?" he whispered. "I got the guy who caused all those fires. Who hurt you."

"He could not wait?" Chiun asked.

"Never mind him. What about you?"

"My end may be near."

"Because of some stupid smoke," Remo said loudly. "I don't believe it."

"I knew this was a mistake," Dr. Gale said. She tried to pull Remo away from the bedside. She took his shoulders in her firm doctor's hands. The shoulders did not budge. They might as well have been set in concrete.

"Sir. I'll have to ask you to step over here. I must speak with you."

Remo came erect with a stricken look on his face.

"What's wrong with him?" Remo hissed when they were on the other side of the room.

"I don't know. We performed every kind of test known to medical science. His blood has been analyzed. We put him through a CAT scan. Ultrasound. Everything. We can find nothing wrong with him physically."

"Then he's going to be okay?"

"No. I'm sorry to tell you that your friend is dying."

"You just said he was fine."

"He's an unbelievable human specimen. Not just for his age, but for any age. My God, do you know that his body is perfectly bisymmetrical?"

"Is that bad?"

"It's incredible. Even in normal people one leg is usually longer than the other. Right-handed people usually have weaker musculature in their left arms, and of course vice versa. In women, it's not uncommon for one breast to be larger. But not this man.

His arms and legs are exactly the same respective lengths. His muscles are perfectly balanced. Even his bone structure is unnaturally symmetrical."

"But what does it mean?"

"It means," said Dr. Gale seriously, "that his body is perfectly proportioned. Perfectly."

Remo nodded. Sinanju. It balanced everything.

"I looked it up in the medical records. There's never been any recorded example of absolute human bisymmetry. I don't want to be precipitate, but I have here a standard medical donor form. If you would consider willing the body to science, I can assure you that the utmost respect will be paid to the remains."

Remo took the form and silently folded it into a delta-winged paper airplane. He sailed it past Dr. Gale's ear. It seemed to just tap a wall mirror, but the glass spiderwebbed with a brittle *crack*!

"My goodness!" Dr. Gale said.

"I want some answers, or I'll start folding you next."

Dr. Gale fingered her shiny new stethoscope and chose her next words carefully.

"As I told you, sir, we can find nothing organically wrong with the dear sweet man. But his life signs are definitely failing. It's not his heart, and although we suctioned smoke traces from his lungs, they don't appear to be damaged either. But all indications are that he is simply . . . expiring."

"Chiun can't simply die. It doesn't work that way with him. It can't."

"The finest medical equipment does not lie. We can't explain it. He's obviously healthy, yet he's clearly dying. He is very old. It does happen to some people this way. But usually they go quick. In Mr. Chiun's case, it's as if his soul, his magnificent soul, is outgrowing his frail old body."

"Well put," said Chiun from his bed.

"Thank you," Dr. Gale said sweetly. She turned back to Remo. "As you can see, he's fully aware of his condition. He doesn't seem disturbed at all. I think he knows that his time has come, and he's just awaiting the end. Personally, I think it's a beautiful way to go. I hope I'm this lucky."

"How long?" Remo asked hoarsely. It was just starting to sink in.

"A few weeks. Possibly a month. He's asking for you to take him home. I think that would be best. There's obviously nothing we can do further. Take him home, and make him comfortable."

"There's no hope?"

"None whatsoever. People his age—when they get sick, even from minor ailments—they almost never fully recover. He seems to be able to accept that. You should too."

Remo returned to Chiun's bedside. Chiun seemed smaller somehow, as if his great essence had shriveled within the frail husk that was his body.

"Little Father, I will take you back to Folcroft with me."

"Do not be silly, Remo," Chiun said quietly. "That is no place for a Master of Sinanju to spend his last days. We will enjoy them in Sinanju . . . together."

"Are you sure it's this bad?"

"Remo, I will not deceive you on this. I am entering my final days on earth. Inform the Emperor Smith to make the necessary arrangements. I wish to leave the sights and smells of this barbaric land for all time."

"Yes, Little Father," said Remo, and there were tears in his eyes as he left the room.

5

The chill November dawn shone through the huge picture window overlooking Long Island Sound and found Dr. Harold W. Smith still at his desk. He was a tall man, with thinning hair and rimless glasses. His three-piece suit was gray. Almost everything about the man was gray, washed-out and colorless.

But Smith, sitting behind the administrator's desk at Folcroft Sanitarium, was anything but colorless. Next to the President of the United States, he was the most powerful man in the U.S. government. Some might say more powerful, because Presidents came and went, but Harold W. Smith, appointed the sole director of CURE, held forth, unelected and unimpeachable.

Smith tightened his striped Dartmouth tie as he waited for the computer terminal on his desk to process news digests coming from the city of Detroit. Another man, after working through the night, would have long before loosened his tie. But not Smith. He wanted to be presentable when his secretary came to work.

The information from Detroit was good. There were fewer fires this year, and most were under control. But it was odd that no reports regarding one Moe Joakley had surfaced. Odder still that Remo hadn't checked in.

Smith saved the Detroit digests as a separate file and went on to other incoming data. His fingers brushed the keyboard with a concert pianist's unself-conscious ease. The tiny terminal was deceiving. It hooked up to a bank of computers in a sealed room in Folcroft's basement. These linked up to virtually every data base in the United States, and a few elsewhere. They scanned all computer traffic automatically, sifting through data transmissions for indications of criminal or unusual activity. Twenty years of CURE data base lay stored in its secret files, a backup data base in another secret computer bank on the island of St. Martin. If Remo was the enforcement arm of CURE, and Smith was its brain, the CURE computers were its heart.

Before Remo, Smith had fought his own private war through his computers, sifting computer links for tipoffs to improper stock transactions, large bank transfers that might reveal bribes received or the movement of drug money. Through unsuspected connections to the IRS and Social Security Administration files, he possessed unmatchable identification facilities. An army of informants in all walks of life reported to Smith through these computers, never suspecting they were reporting to an unknown organization called CURE. In the pre-Remo days, Smith anonymously tipped off the proper law-enforcement agencies to crimes in the making. Now he did that with only the routine problems. On the big stuff he sent in Remo Williams.

It was illegal, of course, but CURE was not a legal entity. Just a necessary one. Data streamed into Smith's computer, were sorted and tagged. Criminal patterns, aberrations in money and stock transfers, in arms and goods, triggered red flags built into the software. Important criminal activity in the making was thus targeted and offered to Smith as a probability readout, for possible action.

With the end in sight, Smith could see a day when more of his work would return to those days before he had ordered Remo Williams pressed into CURE's service. Maybe ordinary law-enforcement agencies could take up the burden. For a brief second Smith thought about retirement, then dismissed it.

There could be no retirement for a CURE operative. Just death. Near the basement computer bank there was a coffin with Smith's name on it. It was there in case a presidential directive ordered Smith to disband CURE for security reasons. A secret such as CURE could not be saved for retirement. Smith was prepared to die.

Smith dismissed the thought from his mind. Something was wrong with the computer, the screen was dimming. Brownout.

CURE's computers ran off Folcroft's supposedly dormant backup generators, but they were failing. Smith touched a switch beside the terminal, switching power from the generators to Folcroft's main lines.

The screen brightened.

"Memo to Mrs. Mikulka," Smith said into a pocket memo recorder. "Have the emergency generators overhauled."

The phone rang.

"Harold?" an older woman's voice asked. It was Smith's wife. Even she called him Harold. It was never Harry or Hal.

"Yes, dear?"

"Will you be home for lunch?"

"No. I will be working through the day."

"I worry about you, Harold. Working all night like this."

"Yes, dear," Smith said absently, watching the screen.

"Don't forget to have a good breakfast."

The CURE line began blinking.

"One moment," Smith said. "I have another call." He switched to the other phone, putting his wife on hold.

"Yes, Remo. You were successful?"

"Chiun is dying," Remo blurted out.

Smith said nothing for a long moment.

"You are sure?" he asked carefully.

"Of course I'm sure. Dammit, would I say something like that if I wasn't sure? The doctors say it's so and even Chiun says it's so."

"What's wrong with him?"

"No one knows."

Smith thought Remo sounded close to tears. He said, "I'll arrange a special flight. We'll bring Chiun back to Folcroft. The finest doctors will examine him."

"Forget all that crap. Chiun wants to go home. He says he wants to die there."

"There are no medical facilities in Sinanju," Smith said flatly. "We can do more for him here."

"Look, Chiun wants to go home. So he's going home. Set it up, Smitty!"

"It's not that simple," Smith pointed out with implacable logic. "Chartering a U.S. nuclear sub isn't like calling a cab. The *Darter* is in San Diego being refitted for the annual shipment of gold to Chiun's village. It leaves in two weeks. We'll bring Chiun here and attend to him until the sub is ready."

"We're going to Sinanju, Smitty. Now. Even if I have to steal a plane and fly it myself."

Remo's tone of voice was shocking in its vehemence.

"Very well," Smith said, with more calmness than he felt. "I will arrange a flight to the west coast. A submarine will be waiting at the usual spot. You know the drill."

"Thanks, Smitty," Remo said suddenly.

"I want you back when this is over," Smith said without warmth. "Now, if you'll excuse me, Irma is on the other line."

"Irma? Who's Irma?" Remo asked.

"My wife."

"I thought your wife's name was Maude."

"It is," Smith said evenly. "Irma is her pet name."

"Only you, Smitty, would give a woman named Maude a pet name like Irma," said Remo. "If you had a dog, you'd call it Fido. Or Rover. I'll be in touch."

"Don't forget to come back," Smith said, and hung up.

"You were saying, dear," Smith said into the other phone.

"I said don't forget to have a good breakfast."

"Yes, dear. Mrs. Mikulka always brings my unsweetened grapefruit juice and prune-whip yogurt from the commissary when she somes in."

"Good. I'll see you at dinner." The line went dead.

Smith returned to his computer. He began keying in the commands that would, through people in the United States military, initiate the movements of aircraft that would evacuate Remo and Chiun to Miramar Naval Air Station in California, and from there by helicopter to the USS. *Darter*, stationed at the San Diego Naval Base. The sub would require emergency orders from COMSUBPAC to leave its station early, but Smith could accomplish that by remote control.

He had that power. And no one knew it.

Colonel Viktor Ditko pored over a map of North Korea and found Sinanju on the west coast. It was on a bay at the edge of one of the most heavily industrialized sectors of the North. A tiny dot indicated the location.

Going to a more detailed map, Ditko found, to his dismay, that only another tiny dot indicated Sinanju's location.

He swore under his breath. North Korean maps. They were no more reliable than North Koreans.

Ditko dug out a map so detailed that it showed city blocks in the nearby towns of Chonju and Sunchon. Sinanju was simply a blank area at the edge of Sinanju Bay.

"Do they not have streets in Sinanju?" he asked himself.

Colonel Ditko got on the phone. He called his liaison in the North Korean government.

"Captain Nekep speaking," said an oily voice.

"I must ask you a question. You must not repeat this question to anyone."

"Done," said Captain Nekep, who had been a lowly corporal until Colonel Ditko tipped him off to a planned assassination attempt against North Korea's Great Leader, Kim Il Sung. As a result, Nekep had been promoted and Colonel Ditko had a potentially valuable ally in the North Korea Army.

"What do you know of Sinanju?" Ditko asked.

"On our official maps, it is designated as a restricted area with a double red line."

Ditko whistled soundlessly. The Presidential Palace in Pyongyang rated only a single red line.

"It is a military installation, then?"

"No. It is a fishing village."

"Does it not seem strange to you, Captain, that a mere fishing village is kept off limits?"

"I do not ask questions about matters when to know the answer carries a hanging penalty."

"I need to get a person into Sinanju."

"I do not know you," said Captain Nekep, and hung up.

"Ingrate," Colonel Ditko hissed. But the captain's reaction had satisfied him that the videotape recording made by the Korean-American journalist Sammy Kee was indeed valuable.

He would take the tape to Moscow personally. It was risky, but great rewards might result from the taking of such a risk. And Colonel Viktor Ditko had known disgrace in his career. He did not fear it.

In the basement of the Russian embassy, Colonel Ditko unlocked the interrogation room, which he had ordered off limits.

Sammy Kee awoke with a start. He had been sleeping on a mat. He slept a lot. At first, he couldn't sleep from nervous exhaustion, but after a day and a half of captivity, depression had set in like a nagging cold. He slept a lot when he was depressed. It was a blessing now.

"Get up," Colonel Ditko ordered.

Sammy got up, rubbing the sleep from his eyes.

"Listen to me. Here is food and water and a bowl for your bodily functions. I will not be able to let you out to go to the bathroom for at least three days. Do not fear that I have abandoned you. I am going to Moscow, to speak with the General Secretary personally. In the meantime, you will stay locked within this room. I am taking the only key with me. Do not cry for help. Do not call attention to yourself. I am the only person in the compound who knows you are here. If others find you, your death would be certain."

"I understand," said Sammy Kee dully.

"You are a long way from San Francisco," Colonel Ditko reminded him.

"I know."

"Good. I will return within three days."

"What if you don't?"

"It will be better for you to starve to death in this room than if you are discovered. You know that?"

And Sammy Kee slipped to the floor as the door locked shut.

It was sound psychology, Colonel Ditko knew. The Korean-American might hate him and fear him, and that would be useful later. But for the next few days, Sammy Kee would live for Colonel Ditko's return, because Ditko's return meant fresh food and relief from the claustrophobic smell of his own excrement.

It was so easy to manipulate these soft Americans, Colonel Ditko thought to himself. In his home environment, Sammy Kee would not think twice about his next meal. Bathroom facilities he took for granted. Colonel Ditko had made them more important than anything else—including Sammy Kee's desire to escape. That would safeguard his own secret until he returned to North Korea.

Returning to his own quarters, Colonel Viktor Ditko removed his glasses and dropped them to the hardwood floor. They did not shatter. So he crushed them under the heel of his boot.

Picking up the largest shard of one lens, Colonel Ditko walked to his bunk. In the Soviet KGB there were no transfers home, not by request or bribe. Only for medical emergency.

But Colonel Ditko had to get back to Moscow. And so, he sat on his bunk and, steeling himself, slowly sliced the pupil of his left eye with a piece of broken eyeglass.

The rewards, he told himself as he ground his teeth in agony, would be worth the pain.

6

"Little Father, are you comfortable?" Remo asked tenderly.

Chiun, Master of Sinanju, lay on a reed mat on the floor of the submarine cabin. They had been given the largest officers' stateroom, which meant that, with the folding bunk up, it was slightly more spacious than a pantry. Two fluffy pillows cradled Chiun's aged head. His hazel eyes were dreamy, half-closed.

"I will be comfortable when this voyage is at last over."

"Me too," said Remo, kneeling beside Chiun. The room pitched ever so slightly. Incense curled from brass bowls Remo had placed in every corner of the cabin to smother the stale metallic taste of the recirculated air that was inescapable on even the most modern nuclear submarine. Remo had spent half the afternoon covering the false wood paneling of the walls with tapestries from the fourteen steamer trunks that contained Chiun's personal possessions.

"The captain said we should be arriving before evening," Remo said.

"How would he know? There is no evening in this filthy vessel."

"Hush," said Remo, trying to soothe Chiun's mood. "We were lucky that this sub was ready to go."

"Did you check the gold, as I asked?"

"Twice in the last hour. It is safe."

"It is well. This may be the last gold the village of Sinanju will receive from the mad Emperor Smith."

"Don't say that, Chiun."

"Still," Chiun continued, his eyes still half-closed, "I am at peace, for we are going home. To Sinanju."

"You are going home, Little Father. Sinanju is your home, not mine. Smith expects me to return to America."

"How can you return to that land? And leave your wife? Your children? Your village?"

Remo forgot himself and asked, "Wife? Children? What are you babbling about?"

"Why, the wife you will take once we are in Sinanju. And the children she will bear you. It is your duty, Remo. When I am gone, you must carry on the traditions. And Sinanju must have an heir."

"I am honored, Little Father, but I don't know that I can do that."

"Do not be shy, Remo. If you cannot find a Sinanju maiden who will accept your whiteness, I will find one for you. I promise."

"Oh no," said Remo. "Not more matchmaking. Remember what happened last time you tried to fix me up with a Korean girl? I'm not going through that again."

"I am dying, without a true heir, bereft of grandchildren, and you are burdening me with your childish concerns."

"I am sorry you do not have grandchildren, Little Father. I cannot help that."

"Perhaps if you hurry, I will live long enough to see your bride fat with child. I could go peacefully into the Void then. That would be enough. It is not the same as bouncing a grandchild on my knee, but I have been cursed by misfortune all my life."

"You've made more money from America's contract than all of the Masters in Sinanju history combined."

"I have not gotten respect. I have not worked for a true emperor, but for a doctor, and a quack at that. In Egypt, the court physician always walked a full two paces behind the royal assassin. Now we are reduced to working for bloodletters."

"The village can live comfortably for centuries on the stuff in your treasure house."

"How many times have I instructed you that Masters of Sinanju do not touch capital?" Chiun demanded. "I am the first Master to change his name in shame. Have I told you that story, Remo?"

Remo started to say yes, but Chiun was already into the tale.

"I was not always known as Chiun. I was born Nuihc, son of Nuihc, grandson of Yui. My line was a proud line, for I was the bearer of the great tradition of Sinanju. But my house fell on hard times. First there were the terrible European wars that blanketed the world, when there was no proper work for the assassin. Just for foot soldiers. My prime years were spent in idleness and inglorious tasks.

"I married unwisely. For my wife, who was sharp of tongue and avaricious of nature, bore me no heirs. This was a tragedy, but not without salvation. At her insistence, I agreed to train as the next Master of Sinanju a nephew, also named, after me, Nuihc. I trained him in the sun source. He was a good pupil. He learned slowly, but he learned thoroughly. Unlike some."

Remo didn't know if that last was a dig or a left-handed compliment. He let it pass.

"When the day came that I stepped down as Master of Sinanju, Nuihc went off on his first task. The days passed in silence, they turned to weeks, and months. And when years passed, I heard how this Nuihc, this fat-faced deceiver, was practicing Sinanju willy-nilly all over the world. Not a dram of tribute came back to the village of Sinanju. It looked as if hard times were back, and soon we would be sending the babies home to the sea."

Remo nodded. Sending the babies home to the sea meant drowning them. The Village of Sinanju was poor, the soil unplantable, the waters of the bay too frigid to yield food fish. In olden times, when there wasn't enough food for everyone, the babies were drowned in the cold bay in the hope that they would be reborn in a better time. First the girls, then, as a last resort, the boys. In Sinanju, they called it "sending the babies home to the sea" to ease the pain of the terrible necessity.

"And so," Chiun continued, "at an age when Masters before me were happily retired from world travel and raising many grandchildren, I again took up the responsibility of my ancestors. In my shame, I reversed the letters of my name, Nuihc, so that none would think I was related to the base traitor, also called Nuihc. And I became Chiun. So I was known when we first met, Remo."

Remo remembered. It was in Folcroft's gymnasium. It seemed like a long time ago. Chiun was the trainer MacCleary and Smith had picked to transform Remo into CURE's killer arm. At first, Chiun merely taught Remo karate, a little Ninjutsu, and some other light skills. But after a few weeks, Chiun suddenly told Remo to forget everything he had learned up till then.

"Child's games," Chiun had whispered. "Tricks stolen from my ancestors by thieves. They are the rays of the sun source. Sinanju is the source. I will now teach you Sinanju."

And so it had begun.

"I remember when MacCleary first came to my village," Chiun continued in a faraway voice. "I had again retired, this time for lack of employment. MacCleary asked for something no one had asked for in many centuries. He asked, not for the Master of Sinanju's service, but for his help training another in the sun source. In more plentiful times, I would have slain him where he stood just for suggesting such a thing. But those were not plentiful times. And so I agreed, shamed as I was."

"You weren't sorry long, Little Father." Remo smiled. "I took to Sinanju better than anyone before."

"Silence," said Chiun, this time opening his eyes. "Who is telling this story? You or I? And if you were a good pupil—which I do not admit—it is only because you had perfection for a teacher."

"Excuse me," Remo said, but he was secretly glad. Chiun seemed to be coming out of his half-drowse. There was a little of the old fire in his eyes again, and it made Remo's heart rise.

"This MacCleary told me I would be training an orphan, one who had been found in a basket on a doorstep. I was pleased to hear this. The younger they are the better they absorb Sinanju."

Chiun turned his face to Remo.

"Imagine my disgust when I learned you were fully grown, except in mind."

"You got over it," Remo said gently.

"What I did not get over was your whiteness. I could have trained another Korean. Even a Chinese or a Filipino. Any properly colored person. But a white—worse, an American white of uncertain parentage. I nearly went home when I first cast eyes upon you. That was when I decided to teach you karate and other lesser arts stolen from Sinanju. Who would know the difference?"

"I did."

"No, you did not. But MacCleary knew. He knew of the legends. He understood. I should have trained him."

"You don't believe that, Little Father. Too much has gone on between us."

"Too much for me to understand your ingratitude. You think that Sinanju is just killing? Just fun, fun, fun? How typically white to eat of the fruit and neglect to return the seeds to soil so that others might enjoy the goodness of it in a later season. One grandson. It is all I ask. Is that too much? Even Nuihc would have given me that."

"We got him, though, didn't we?"

"And soon I will join him, unhonored, without assurance that my line will continue."

"Let's talk about it later," Remo said. "Would you like some rice?"

"I am too shamed to eat."

"I'm going to make some anyway," Remo said pleasantly.

"I would choke on the grains."

"White or brown?" asked Remo.

"Brown. I have sworn off all white things," said Chiun, and closed his eyes again.

Captain Lee Enright Leahy had made the run from San Diego to Sinanju harbor every November for more than a dozen years. He had once kept a log of every trip in his personal diary in case the truth behind his missions ever came out and he had the chance to write his memoirs. But after his wife had pointed out that Captain Leahy had somehow aged ten years each November, he stopped counting. He didn't want to know. He was only fifty-five, but he looked seventy.

But who wouldn't look seventy, if once a year he

had to command the United States submarine *Darter* on a suicide mission? It might have helped Captain Leahy's peace of mind if someone had told him what it was all about. But no one ever did. In the early days, Leahy had assumed it was a CIA operation. Then after the Congress had reined in the CIA in the mid-1970's, the operation continued undisturbed. In fact, it had loosened up. The *Darter* no longer had to run across the Pacific at flank bell speed and take all kinds of evasive action off the coast of China to reach the Yellow Sea. The fix was in, Captain Leahy knew. That made it an NSC operation. Had to be. Only the cowboys at the National Security Council could pull off something this big once a year like clockwork.

But it was crazier this year. The *Darter* was being refitted for the mission when emergency orders came in: ship out a week early. It was an impossible order. But the cargo was loaded and ready. All Captain Leahy had to do was recall the crew, who were scattered to the four winds. Captain Leahy had never seen such a mobilization. He would have thought World War III was about to break out. Instead, two civilians were airlifted to the sub under cover of darkness. A Caucasian and an elderly Korean. Leahy assumed the old one was Korean. They were bound for Korea, weren't they? Leahy had seen them both before. He had ferried them to North Korea before. Whoever they were, they were VIP's with two V's— Very, Very Important People.

On this run, as on the previous crossings, the pair stayed in their stateroom. They even cooked their own food there. Captain Leahy had once sent them a couple of London-broil steaks from his personal larder. The steaks were found in the trash-disposal unit on the leg home. Were they afraid of being poisoned?

Entering Control, Captain Leahy wondered, for

the thousandth time, who they were. His wildest imaginings didn't even come close to the truth.

"We've reached Point Sierra, sir," the executive officer told him, giving the code name for their destination. It snapped him out of his glassy-eyed reverie.

"Captain of the Watch, rig controls for black and prepare to surface," Captain Leahy barked.

"Aye aye, sir."

The scarlet illumination lights in the control room winked out. Only the eerie glow of the control indicators shone.

The *Darter* broke surface two miles off the North Korean coast. The Yellow Sea was cold, gray, and running high. It always ran high at this time of year, which was probably the reason the dropoff was always in November.

"Pop hatches," he said, getting ready to climb out on deck. "Get the rafts ready."

Dressed in oils, Captain Leahy stood on the icy upper deck trying to keep his teeth from chattering. Cold waves crashed against the conning sail, sending needles of spray into the air.

It had been years since Leahy had to land the gold in the rocky Korean harbor by frogmen. Now they let him surface off the North Korean coast and land the cargo by rubber raft. NSC for sure, he said to himself. The fix was in. But the knowledge didn't relieve his peace of mind one whit. He remembered what had happened to the crew of the *Pueblo* so many years ago, when they had been captured in North Korean waters.

Captain Leahy conned the distant shore with his binoculars. The horizon was a broken line of rocks. But he was looking for two rocks in particular, the formation that his original orders called the Horns of Welcome.

When Captain Leahy spotted the Horns of Welcome, he sent word below.

"Tell the passengers we're here."

"Where?" asked his officer of the deck, who was new to this operation.

"Don't ask. I looked at a map of North Korea once. I think we're off the shore of a place called Sinanju."

"What is it?"

"Sinanju. That's all I was able to learn."

"Tells you a lot."

"It's more than we should know."

Two sailors brought the old Korean up the weapons-shipping hatch in a strap-in stretcher. Once topside, they undid the webbing restraints and transferred him to a wicker wheelchair. The Caucasian issued the orders.

"Be careful with him."

The old Korean looked like a pale wrinkled mummy, as if he were near death. But when one of the sailors carrying the cargo—five crates of gold ingots—tripped over his own feet and dropped one crate, the old man's long-nailed hand seemed to drift out and lightly touch the offending crewman's right elbow.

"Be careful with that, white!" the Korean hissed.

The sailor grabbed his elbow and went into a dance like a man who had stuck his tongue into a wall socket.

The crewman had to be replaced while the crates were loaded onto five collapsible motor dinghies, each manned by one sailor.

Next came the fourteen lacquered steamer trunks. They were loaded into rubber rafts, one for each trunk.

Finally, the Oriental was gently set in another raft, and the Caucasian got in with him.

"My God, this looks like a beach-assault operation," the officer of the deck groaned. "What happens if a North Korean destroyer stumbles across us?"

"It happened once, two years ago," Captain Leahy said grimly.

"Oh? What happened?"

"They hung around long enough to identify us as American. Then they came about and ran."

"They had us dead to rights and they ran?"

"No. They had us dead to rights *and* dead in the water. We were sitting ducks. That's when they ran."

"My God, what kind of operation is this?"

"I don't know, but my guess is we're making some kind of history here."

"I hope I live long enough to read about it," the officer of the deck whispered.

"Me too," Captain Leahy said fervently. He watched the progress of the rafts through his binoculars. Half the time they were invisible in the choppy seas. He waited. It was a bad place to wait.

When the boats at last returned, empty, the leader of the landing party climbed aboard.

"Mission accomplished, sir!" he said, saluting.

"Excellent. Now let's get the hell out of this place."

"Until next year, anyway," the officer of the deck said.

"Shut up, mister," Captain Lee-Enright Leahy snapped. "You may be here next year, but I won't. They've got me up for early retirement. I just hope I have enough good years left in me to enjoy them."

7

The package arrived in the office of the General Secretary of the Union of Soviet Socialist Republics at ten-thirty in the morning. It was addressed to the General Secretary personally and carried the following warning, in letters of the Cyrillic alphabet: "FOR THE EYES OF THE GENERAL SECRETARY ONLY. IMPORTANT SECRET ENCLOSED.

Mysterious packages did not often come to the Kremlin's bustling mailroom. The package was immediately placed in a lead-lined bucket and sent by dumbwaiter—a relic from czarist days—to a basement bunker.

There, a team of explosives-disposal experts placed it under a fluoroscope. The X ray revealed the ghostly outlines of a rectangular box containing what appeared to be two coils. That was enough for them to bring in the dogs.

They sent in the German shepherds, specially trained to scent explosives. While the dogs sniffed the package, their trainers hunkered down behind a five-foot-thick concrete buttress.

When, after five minutes, the dogs did not howl,

the experts emerged timorously, shedding their protective outfits.

"It appears to be harmless," muttered the head of the team.

"What if you are wrong?" asked the second member of the team.

"Then we will be wrong."

"*You* will sign the certificate of safety then, comrade."

"Then I alone will get the credit."

"I will sign the certificate also," said the third member of the team, who was in charge of the dogs.

They all signed the certificate and the package was run up the dumbwaiter to the office of the General Secretary.

The secretary to the General Secretary brought the package in to her superior.

"I did not open it, Comrade General Secretary," she said.

The General Secretary regarded the package. His high forehead wrinkled in perplexity, sending the wine-colored birthmark that rode high on his skull into convulsions. There was no return address on the outside of the package.

"You did well. Now leave me."

The General Secretary slit the edge of the package, which was of reinforced cardboard, with a letter opener and undid the end flap.

Out popped a black video cassette wrapped in a copy of *Izvestia*. Within the page was a thick sheaf of pages, closely typed. There was also a note, handwritten.

The note read:

General Secretary,

This tape contains information of global import. I beg you to watch it in solitude. Enclosed is a transcript of the person speaking on the tape,

first in his native language, then in English, and
again in Russian. The Russian transcript is mine.

If you wish to speak to me on this serious matter, I am in the Military Ward of the Kremlin
Clinic.

> Yours faithfully,
> Viktor Ditko,
> Colonel, Committee of State Security

The General Secretary buzzed his personal secretary—"Do not disturb me for the next hour"—and
went into the adjoining conference room where there
was an American-made video cassette recorder. He
watched the tape in deep silence, transcript in hand.

When he was done, his face was two degrees paler.
His cranial birthmark, by contrast, was livid. He
grabbed for the intercom like an alcoholic.

"I wish to know the status of a KGB colonel cur-
rently being treated at the Kremlin Clinic."

The secretary came back with a verbal report:

"Comrade General Secretary, Colonel Viktor Ditko
is awaiting an eye operation, and is considered under arrest for possible dereliction of duty."

"The specific charge?"

"That he deliberately caused severe injury to his
eye in order to avoid duty." The secretary wore a
disapproving expression when she gave the report.

"His station?"

"Head of security, Soviet embassy, Pyongyang, People's Democratic Republic of Korea."

"I will see him in this office, within the hour."

"He has a history of shirking his responsibilities,"
the secretary added.

"He will not shirk this appointment, I assure you."

"As you wish, General Secretary."

* * *

Colonel Viktor Ditko smiled as he was ushered into the baroque office of the General Secretary. He looked pale. His uniform was not fully pressed. The General Secretary took his measure. Ditko appeared to be a dull, studious sort, not very personable in appearance, but there was a hint of cunning in his eyes. Or rather, in the one eye that was not covered by a black eyepatch. The rakish look that eyepatches normally give a man was undercut and made incongruous by the horn-rimmed glasses he wore.

The General Secretary waved him to a chair without a word.

"Thank you, Comrade General Secretary," said Colonel Ditko. He looked overimpressed by his surroundings. The General Secretary thought for a moment that he was going to do something stupid, like bowing from the waist.

"I have watched the tape," the General Secretary said after a long pause.

"It is important, *da?*"

The General Secretary nodded. "It may be. Who has seen this tape aside from you?"

"The person who recorded it. He also prepared the transcripts."

"No one else?"

"I swear. I understand its importance."

"You came by this how?"

And Colonel Viktor Ditko let the story spill out, the words tumbling from his prim mouth so swiftly they ran together and the General Secretary was forced to ask him to slow down.

When it was over, Colonel Ditko said, "I knew I had to get this to you. I dared not send it by diplomatic pouch. I had to inflict an injury upon myself to facilitate my return. My superiors believe I was derelict in my duty. But of course, you know differently."

The General Secretary dismissed the subject of Colonel Ditko's superiors with an impatient wave.

"Your eye. What did the doctors say?"

"Repair is possible. We have excellent eye surgeons in Moscow."

"I will see that you get the best. What do you want from me?"

"Sir?"

"Your reward," asked the General Secretary.

"A better post. One in Moscow."

"You have something in mind?"

Colonel Viktor Ditko hesitated, and the General Secretary began to suspect that the colonel was merely a clever fool. When Colonel Ditko forced the trembling answer out, the General Secretary knew he was a fool.

"The Ninth Directorate. Possibly?"

The General Secretary stifled a laugh. It came out as a explosive grunt and Colonel Ditko wondered if he'd overreached himself.

The Ninth Directorate was responsible for guarding members of the Politburo. The General Secretary could not believe it. The man had risked his career and maimed himself to deliver a secret of such immense import that it promised to tip the balance of power between East and West, and he asked nothing more than to be appointed glorified bodyguard to the Politburo. The man could have had an appointment that would have led, in the course of a half-decent career, to a position on the Politburo itself. Here was a fool.

But the General Secretary did not say that. Instead, he said, "It is possible. Where is the person who taped this?"

"He is a prisoner in our Pyongyang embassy."

"And he is half-Korean. Good. Do you think you can undertake an important mission for your country?"

"At your service, Comrade General Secretary."

"Return to Korea. Send this Sammy Kee back to Sinanju. Get more proof. Better proof. Any proof. Perhaps some of the records in Sinanju, especially any records having to do with America. Bring them to me. I will act on this when I know exactly what cards I am holding. I do not wish to be trumped."

"I will return to Pyongyang directly," said Colonel Viktor Ditko as he got to his feet. "And I promise you success, Comrade General Secretary."

"I expect no less," said the General Secretary dismissively.

As he watched Colonel Viktor Ditko give a crisp salute and turn on his heel, the General Secretary of the Union of Soviet Socialist Republics wondered where in the Ninth Directorate he could bury this fool of a career colonel. He was too much a buffoon to trust with guarding anyone of importance. Perhaps he would assign him to one of his political rivals.

Sammy Kee was more frightened than he'd ever been.

He huddled in a corner of the interrogation room in the basement of the Russian embassy in Pyongyang and breathed through his mouth to keep the stench out of his nostrils. Sometimes he retched. Only by sticking his mouth and nose down into his peasant blouse could he stop the gagging reflex caused by the odor emanating from the big wooden bowl in the far corner.

It had been four days since Colonel Viktor Ditko had locked the door on Sammy Kee. Ditko had said he would be gone only three days. Had something happened? Had Ditko gotten into an accident while driving to the airport? Had his plane crashed? A thousand possibilities ran through Sammy Kee's frightened mind.

Sammy Kee didn't know what to do. He was out of canned food. There was no more water. The room was empty except for the plain table and two old hardwood chairs. He wondered if it was possible to chew wood so that it was digestible. He had never believed a Russian could be so cruel. He wanted to write Peter, Paul, and Mary to tell them.

Heavy footsteps sounded outside the door, and Sammy's heart leapt at the sound. He crawled to the door, as he had at every noise for three days, and pressed his ear to the panel. But no scrape of a key in the lock came. No rattle of a doorknob. Sammy wanted to cry out for someone, anyone. But he didn't. He never did. He wanted to live. More than anything, he wanted to live.

And he knew that, in his position, Colonel Viktor Ditko meant life itself.

As if it would help his predicament, Sammy Kee cursed the day he heard the name of Sinanju. He cursed his grandfather, but he knew it was not his grandfather's fault. His grandfather had been an old broken man. One who should have stayed in Korea. Maybe all of Sammy Kee's family should have stayed in Korea. He cried when he thought of that.

Maybe it would be better in Moscow, Sammy Kee thought. He toyed with the idea, even though deep in his heart he doubted he would ever leave Korea alive. But the human spirit is an unconquerable thing. And so Sammy imagined what it would be like to drink in the bitter cold air of Red Square, to shop at the big Moscow department store, GUM. Or maybe they would let him shop at the Intourist stores, where he could get Western goods at cheaper prices. And then Sammy thought again of San Francisco, and he broke down.

He was still crying when someone rattled the door-knob. The door lock turned. And before Sammy Kee could even begin to register hope or fear, Colonel Viktor Ditko stood in the room, regarding him with a single cold eye.

"Uggh!" Colonel Ditko said, reacting to the wafting stench. "Out, quickly."

And Sammy came running.

Colonel Ditko hustled him into a corner of the basement, beside a creaky roaring furnace.

"I was longer than I expected," the colonel said.

Sammy Kee nodded wordlessly, noting but not asking about the colonel's eyepatch.

"You were not found?"

"No," said Sammy Kee.

"Good. Listen to me, Sammy Kee. I have been to Moscow. I have spoken to a great man, perhaps the greatest leader in the world. He has seen your tape and he says it is not enough. Not enough to give you asylum, nor to pay you money."

Sammy Kee gave out a great racking sob.

"I have betrayed my country for nothing," he blubbered.

"Do not fold on me now. This is not over. You are a brave man, Sammy Kee."

But Sammy Kee was not listening. He seemed about to faint.

Colonel Ditko shook Sammy's shoulder violently.

"Listen to me. You are a brave man. You entered this fortress country on your own initiative. And when you were discovered you had the presence of mind to seek the only safe haven open to a Westerner trapped in North Korea. Dig down into yourself and dredge up that bravery again. It, and only it, will save you now."

"I will do anything you ask," said Sammy Kee at last.

"Good. Where is your video equipment?"

"I buried it in the sand. Near Sinanju."

"With extra tapes?"

"Yes."

"I am sending you back to Sinanju. Today. Now. I will see that you have safe conduct to the closest place. From there, you can get back to the village, *nyet?*"

"I don't want to go back there."

"Choice does not enter into it," Ditko said coldly. "I am sending you back to Sinanju. There you will obtain further proof of the Master of Sinanju and his American connection, if you have to steal the very records of Sinanju. You will bring them back to me. Do you understand? Do you?"

"Yes," said Sammy Kee dully.

"You will bring back to me all the secrets of the Master of Sinanju. All of them. And when you do this, you shall be rewarded."

"I will live in Moscow?"

"If you wish. Or we can send you back to America."

"I can't go back there. I've betrayed my country."

"Fool. Do not let your guilt confuse you. No one knows this. And even if word of your perfidy should leak out, it will not matter. You have stumbled upon a secret so embarrassing to the American government that they would not dare prosecute you."

And for the first time, Sammy Kee smiled. It was all going to work out. He could almost see the Golden Gate Bridge in his mind's eye.

8

When the last of the *Darter's* crew had paddled their rafts back out into the forbidding coldness of Sinanju harbor, Remo Williams stood on the rocky shore between the Horns of Welcome, which were also recorded in the history of the House of Sinanju as the Horns of Warning.

Remo looked around. There was no welcoming party, but the two men had not been expected.

Remo adjusted the flannel blanket that covered the Master of Sinanju's lap, tucking the corners into the wicker wheelchair.

"Don't worry, Little Father," Remo said tenderly. "I'll get the villagers down here to help with the gold."

"No," said Chiun. "They must not see me like this. Help me to my feet, Remo."

"You can't get up," said Remo. "You're ill."

"I may be ill, but I am still the Master of Sinanju. I do not want the people of my village to see me like this. They might lose heart. Assist me to my feet."

Reluctantly Remo stripped the blanket free.

Chiun eased himself up like an arthritic. Remo took him by the arm and helped him to his feet.

"Dispose of that thing," said Chiun. "I will not look at it again."

Remo shrugged. "Whatever you say, Little Father," and he took the wheelchair in both hands and with a half-twist of his body sent it arcing up into the star-sprinkled sky. It splashed into the bay waters far out past the wave line.

Chiun stood, unsteady on his feet, his arms tucked into his voluminous sleeves. He sniffed the air delicately.

"I am home," he intoned. "These are the smells of my childhood and they fill my old heart."

"I smell dead fish," Remo said sourly.

"Silence," commanded the Master of Sinanju. "Do not spoil my homecoming with your white complaints."

"I'm sorry, Little Father," Remo said contritely. "Do you want me to fetch the villagers now?"

"They will come," said Chiun.

"It's the middle of the night. If I know these people, they've been asleep since Tuesday."

"They will come," said Chiun stubbornly.

But they did not come. Remo still wore the turtleneck jersey that concealed his bruised throat. The chill wind off the bay cut through it like a glittering knife. And in response, his body temperature automatically rose, fending off the cold with an internal wave of heat.

Remo felt warmer immediately, but he worried about Chiun, standing proud and barefoot in his purple homecoming robes.

"Little Father," Remo started to say, but Chiun cut him off with a chop of his hand.

"Hark," said Chiun.

"I don't hear anything," said Remo.

"Have you no ears?" demanded Chiun. "Listen to its cry."

And Remo, seeing a flash of white wing in the moonlight, realized what Chiun meant. "It's only a sea gull," he said.

"It is the sea gull of welcome," said Chiun, and putting his lips together, whistled a high, keening call.

Chiun turned to Remo. "I was welcoming him in return," he explained.

A minute later, a dark figure stepped out from behind a barnacle-encrusted boulder. Others followed. They advanced slowly, timidly.

"See?" said Chiun. "I told you they would come."

"I think they're investigating your little *tête-à-tête* with the sea gull."

"Nonsense," said Chiun. "They sensed the awesome magnificence that is the Master of Sinanju, and it has pulled them from their contented sleep."

"Anything you say, Chiun."

The first to approach was an old man, not so old as Chiun. He was taller, and broader of face.

"Hail, Master of Sinanju," the old man intoned in formal Korean, "who sustains the village and keeps the code faithfully. Our hearts cry a thousand greetings of love and adoration. Joyous are we upon the return of him who graciously throttles the universe."

And Chiun bowed in return, whispering to Remo in English, "Take note. This is proper respect, properly paid."

"If you ask me, I think he's unhappy about being woken up," Remo hissed back.

Chiun ignored him.

"Know you now that the sun has at last set upon my evil labors," he replied, also in formal Korean. "I am now come home to drink in the sights of the home village, to hear again the sounds of my youth, and to spend my declining days."

There was a sleepy mutter of approval from the others.

"And I have brought my adopted son, Remo, to carry on the great line of my ancestors," Chiun said expansively.

Silence.

"Behold the tribute I have brought from the land of the round-eyed barbarians," Chiun exclaimed loudly.

The crowd burst into cheering and whistling. They descended upon the crates of gold ingots and, like starved locusts, carried them off.

"Bring the palanquin of the Master," called the old man, who was known as Pullyang, the caretaker.

And swiftly, others approached, bearing a litter of rosewood and ivory, like those in which the pharaohs of old were carried. They set it at Chiun's feet, and Remo helped him in.

"I don't think they like me any more than last time I was here," Remo whispered in English.

"They are overwhelmed by my unexpected return. Do not worry, Remo. I have told them all about you."

"No wonder they hate me," Remo grunted.

"They have changed. You will see."

Remo started to get into the palanquin, but the old man called Pullyang suddenly got in his way and gave a signal.

The palanquin was lifted aloft and swiftly borne inland.

"What about me?" asked Remo, in Korean.

"You may carry the lacquer trunks of the Master," Pullyang said disdainfully, and hurried off after Chiun.

"Thanks a lot," said Remo. He looked back out over the waters of the bay. The United States lay thousands of miles beyond the horizon. Remo wondered when he would see it again, and how he would feel when that day came.

Chiun was home. But where was Remo? Where was home to Remo Williams, who never had a home, never had a family, and was about to lose the only family he had ever enjoyed?

Finally, because Remo didn't want to leave Chiun's belongings behind, he dutifully carried them into the village, one by one.

"I want to see him," Remo growled in Korean.

It was the next morning. Remo had been forced to sleep on the hard cold ground, near a pig pen. They had taken Chiun to the treasure house of Sinanju—a magnificent jewel of rare woods and stones, which had been built by Egyptian architects as a tribute to Sinanju during the reign of Tutankhamen—and he had slept there.

Remo had asked where he could sleep. The assembled villagers shrugged, almost in unison. It looked like a herd reflex.

"No room," said Pullyang, the caretaker. He looked around to the other villagers.

"No room," the others had repeated. And they shrugged again.

Remo said, "Oh yeah? Chiun isn't going to like your version of down-home hospitality. I'm going to tell him."

"No. He sleeps now," said the old man. "He does not look well and we know how to care for him."

And so Remo had found a dry patch of ground in the lee of some rocks, where the biting winds were not so fierce.

"Some homecoming," he had said, before dropping off.

Now, with the sun up, he wanted to see Chiun, and they wouldn't let him.

"He sleeps still," said Pullyang of the placid face.

"Bulldookey, Chiun snores like a goose with a deviated beak. He's quiet, so he's awake, and I want to see him."

The old man shrugged again, but before he could say another word, Chiun's voice emerged from the treasure house. It was weak, but it carried.

Remo barged in. He stopped dead.

"Chiun!" Remo said, aghast.

Chiun was sitting in the middle of the spacious central room, whose walls were covered by the tapestries of forgotten civilizations, but hung three deep like layers of wallpaper. Tapers flamed about him, one to each compass point. Behind him, resting on ivory brackets, was a magnificent sword—the Sword of Sinanju. And all around him was the treasure of Sinanju—jars of precious stones, rare statues, and gold ingots in profusion. They were piled at random, as if in an overcrowded antique shop. But Remo didn't register their magnificence. He saw only Chiun.

Chiun sat in a lotus position, on a teak throne which stood barely three inches off the floor. On his head was the spiky gold crown which Masters of Sinanju had worn since the Middle Ages. At his feet were an open scroll and goose quill resting beside an inkstone. But Remo barely noticed those things. What he noticed was Chiun's kimono.

It was black.

"You look fearful, Remo," said Chiun in a placid voice. "What is it?"

"You are wearing the Robes of Death."

"Should I not?" asked Chiun. "Am I not in my final days?" He looked like a wrinkled yellow raisin wrapped in velvet.

"You shouldn't surrender this easily," Remo said.

"Does the oak cling to its darkening leaves when the autumn comes? Do not be sad, Remo. We are home."

"Right. Your people made me sleep on the ground. I spent half the night fighting off snakes."

Chiun looked shocked. But he said, "It was their gift to you."

"Gift? How is sleeping on a rock a gift?"

"They saw the paleness of your skin and hoped the sun would darken it as you slept."

"At night?" Remo demanded.

Chiun pushed the half-finished scroll to one side. "Sit at my feet, Remo. It tires me to have to look up at you."

Remo sat, hugging his knees in his folded arms.

"I don't belong here, Little Father. You know that."

"You have adopted new dress," Chiun noted, pointing a curving fingernail at Remo's turtleneck jersey.

"Just to cover my throat," Remo said, fingering the turtleneck.

"The bruise. It pains you?"

"It's going away."

"No, it is not going away, it is becoming more blue. Am I correct?"

"Never mind me. Why don't you lie down."

"No, I must hurry to finish my scrolls. I must write the history of Master Chiun, last of the pure line of Sinanju, who will be known as Chiun, the Squanderer of Sinanju."

"Please don't lay that guilt trip on me, Little Father. I can't help not being Korean."

"But you are Sinanju. I have made you Sinanju. I have made you Sinanju with my hands and my heart and my will. Admit this."

"Yes," said Remo truthfully. "I am Sinanju. But not Korean."

"I have provided the foundation. The paint will come later."

Chiun's face suddenly narrowed, his wrinkles growing deeper.

"A penny for your thoughts," Remo joked.

"I am thinking of your throat. The traditional investment garments do not cover the throat."

"Investment? Like in stocks and bonds?"

"No, unthinking one. Not as in stocks and bonds. As in becoming the next Master of Sinanju. I have set the ceremony for noon tomorrow. There will be a feast. The villagers will take you into their hearts and you will take a wife."

"We've been through that. I'm not sure I'm ready."

"Ready?" squeaked Chiun. "Does a plum pick itself? It is not for you to say who is ready. One does not become a Master of Sinanju because *you* are ready, but only when the Master before you has reached his end days."

"Can't we just postpone this a few weeks?" pleaded Remo. "I need time to think."

"You are cruel, Remo. I am failing in spirit and you are being petulant like a child who does not wish to go to school."

Remo said nothing.

"You have always been cruel to me. But lately you have been even crueler than befits an ungrateful white. You do not care that I am dying."

"You know that isn't so."

Chiun held up an admonishing finger. His wispy hair trembled.

"You do not care that I am dying. You told me so yourself."

"When?" demanded Remo.

"In that house. During the fire. Before I, ignoring your base cruelty, rescued your uncaring white pelt."

"I don't remember saying anything like that. And I would never say that to you."

"I will quote your own words. As I lay on the floor, my feeble lungs filling with smoke, I beseeched you for help. 'I am dying. I am an old man, and the breath is leaving my poor body,' I said piteously. You turned your uncaring face from me and said, 'Then die quietly.' Unquote."

"I never said that!" Remo protested.

"Do you accuse the Master of Sinanju of telling an untruth?" Chiun asked evenly.

"I know I did not say that," Remo said sullenly.

"But I heard the words. The voice was not yours, but the words, stinging as a viper's fangs, emerged from your very mouth."

"I don't know . . ."

"If I say it is so, will you believe me?" asked Chiun.

"If you say so, Little Father."

"I will accept that as a white's sloppy way of saying yes," said Chiun. He gathered the rich black folds of his robe together before he spoke again.

"Do you remember the legends of the Masters of Sinanju, my ancestors?"

"Some of them. Not all. I get the names mixed up."

"Do you remember the story of the Great Master Wang?"

"There are a lot of stories about Wang. He was a busy guy."

"But there is one story above all others. Before Wang, Masters of Sinanju were not as they are now."

"I know. They fought with sticks and knives and used poison."

"True. And they did not work alone. They had an army of followers, the night tigers of Sinanju. Since Wang, there have been no night tigers. No night tigers were needed. Why is that, Remo?"

"Because Wang was the first to learn the sun source."

"Indeed. It was a terrible time for the House of Sinanju. Wang's Master, who was known as Hung, had died before fully training Wang. It would have been the end of our way of life."

Chiun's voice took on the quavering bass that he used whenever repeating one of the legends of Sinanju.

"And lo, no sooner was the Master Hung cold in the ground than a great sadness descended upon the village of Sinanju. There was work, but there was no Master capable of redeeming the village. The night tigers of Sinanju grew lean with hunger. And they stole from the common villagers. And they killed. And they raped. And they did all manner of evil because their hands were idle and killing was all they knew.

"And Wang, seeing this, betook himself into the darkness to meditate. 'Woe is the House of Sinanju,' Wang said to the night sky. 'For our line is over.'

"And as he lay on the cold earth, lay on his back with his face turned up to the universe, he saw the stars wheeling in their slow course. These stars were cold, remote, and yet they burned like tiny suns. They were eternal. Not like men. But Wang, who had no hope, dared to dream of a time when men were like stars, cold but burning like an inner light. Immortal. 'If only men were like that,' thought Wang, 'our misfortunes would end.'

"Now some say that what transpired next occurred only in the mind of Wang, who had been without food for many days. Others say that it was his fast which opened his eyes to a greater truth. But all agree that when Master Wang returned to Sinanju, he was a different man, cold, remote, and in his eyes burned the fire of the universe.

"For as Wang told it, a great ring of fire descended from the heavens. And lo, this fire burned with a brilliance greater than the sun. And it spoke to Wang. And in a voice that only Wang could hear, it said that men did not use their minds and bodies as they should. And the fire taught Wang the first lesson of control, and in an instant, Wang had found the sun source."

"Sounds like the sun source found *him*," Remo said.

"Hush! And lo, it was a different Wang who returned to Sinanju that night. Tall he stood, and full of wrath. And he found the night tigers of Sinanju plotting against him, saying that this one or that one should become the next Master, for Wang was no more fit than the lowliest of them.

"Into the cooking fires of the village stepped Wang, unharmed by the flames though they lapped at his bare legs. And in a voice like the thunder of an earthquake, he said unto them:

" 'Lo, I am the new Master of Sinanju. I bring with me a new light and a new era, for I have discovered the sun source. No more will there be many Masters. From this day forward, only one Master and one pupil will be worthy to learn the art of Sinanju. No more will there be suffering and hunger. No more will it be necessary for other men of the village to fight and die.'

"And saying those words, the Master Wang, who we now call the Great Master Wang, fell upon the night tigers of Sinanju. And *thak, thak, thak*, these carrion were no more.

"And standing amid the dead, he proclaimed that from this day forward, the mightiest hand of Sinanju would never be raised against one who was of the village. And then he made a prophecy, though not even Wang knew whence his words had come. And he said:

" 'One day there will be a Master of Sinanju who will find among the barbarians in the West one who was once dead. This Master will be so enamored of money that for great wealth he will teach the secrets of Sinanju to this pale one with the dead eyes. He will make him a night tiger, but the most awesome of night tigers. He will make him kin to the gods of India, and he will be Shiva, the Destroyer; Death, the shatterer of worlds. And this dead night tiger whom the Master of Sinanju will one day make whole will himself become the Master of Sinanju, and a new era will dawn, greater than any I am about to create.' "

Chiun sat back in his teak throne, his eyes shining with a beatific light.

"You, Remo," he said softly.

"I know the legend," Remo said. "You told it to me many times. I'm not sure I believe it."

"Do you remember the day you died?" asked Chiun.

"They strapped me in the electric chair. But it didn't work."

Chiun shook his head. "A sham death. It has no meaning. No. I mean that time after your training had begun. A coward attacked you with a pistol. You were not yet one with Sinanju, so he succeeded."

"I remember. You brought me back to life somehow," Remo said.

"I was prepared to let you die. I brought you back only because, in death, your body had aligned itself with the universe. You had taken Sinanju to your heart, as none since Wang had. I could not let you die, though you were white and ungrateful."

"That's when you started thinking I was the fulfillment of that freaking legend?" Remo asked.

"Yes, But it was not until much later that I was certain. It was in China. Do you remember our time in China?"

Remo nodded, wondering where all this was going.

"Yeah. It was one of our earliest assignments. We were there to stop a conspiracy against the opening of diplomatic relations between the U.S. and China. It seems like a long time ago."

"A moment in history," Chiun said. "Do you remember how the deceivers in Peking poisoned you?"

"Yeah, I almost died."

"The poison was enough to kill ten men—no, twenty men. But you did not die. Near death, between death, surrounded by your assassins, you vomited up the poison, and so you lived. That's when I knew for a certainty that you were the true avatar of Shiva the Destroyer."

"Because I upchucked?"

"Many are the tales of Shiva," said Chiun calmly, ignoring Remo's outburst. "There was a time in the days before man when the gods of India were at war with demons. The gods of India were strong, but stronger still were the forces they battled. And so the gods took the great serpent called Vasuki and used him to churn the ocean of milk, for to make ambrosia which the gods would drink and so become more powerful. But the serpent called Vasuki, hanging upside down, began to vomit forth poison into the ocean of milk. And the gods, seeing this, knew that Vasuki's poison would contaminate the ambrosia and deprive them of the strength they needed to ensure victory and their continued existence.

"And lo, down descended Shiva, the red god of storms. Now, Shiva was a terrible god. Three faces had he. Six was the number of his arms. Great might had he. And when he saw the poison vomit forth, he stepped under the serpent called Vasuki and caught the awful poison in his mouth. And so Shiva sacrificed himself to save the world.

"But he did not die, Remo. His wife, who was called Parvati, seeing her consort sacrifice himself, flew swiftly to his side, and before Shiva could swallow the poison, she wrapped a scarf about his throat, strangling it, until Shiva vomited up the poison."

"She strangled him so he wouldn't die of poisoning," Remo said. "That doesn't make any sense."

"Shiva did not die," Chiun corrected. "He vomited up the poison and Parvati undid her scarf. Shiva was unharmed, but for his throat."

Chiun leaned forward and with both hands pushed the collar of Remo's jersey down to expose his throat.

"His throat had turned a bright blue. Like your throat, Remo."

"Coincidence," Remo said, standing up suddenly.

"You persist in your unbelief in the face of overwhelming evidence?"

"I don't have six arms," Remo pointed out. "So I can't be Shiva."

"If those who have died amid the fury of your attack were to stand before us, they would swear that you possessed six times six arms," Chiun said.

Doubt crossed Remo's face. "I've got only one face that I know of," he said finally.

"And how many times has the Emperor Smith altered your face for his own devious purposes?"

"Once when I first joined the organization, so I wouldn't look like my old self," Remo said slowly, counting on his fingers. "Once to cover our tracks after an assignment, and one last time when I made him give me my old face back."

Remo looked at the number of fingers he had counted with surprise.

"Three," said Chiun, raising his eyes to the ceiling.

"You see, the legends are but pretty songs that conceal the true reality, like paint on a woman's face."

"If I were a god, I wouldn't come back to earth as a Newark cop," Remo shot back, almost angrily. "I know that much."

"You are not a Newark cop now. You are something greater. Soon, perhaps, you will take an even greater step toward your ultimate destiny."

"It doesn't add up."

"When you were a child, did you imagine yourself a Newark cop?" asked Chiun. "Children cannot comprehend their inevitable maturity. They do not think past today's desires. You are still like a child in many ways, Remo. But soon you will have to grow up."

The Master of Sinanju bowed his head, and added in a wan voice, "Sooner than I would have thought."

Remo returned to his place at Chiun's feet.

"Sometimes I hear a voice in my head," he admitted. "It's not my voice."

"And what does this voice say?" asked Chiun.

"Sometimes it says, 'I am Shiva. I burn with my own light.' Other times, 'I am created Shiva, the Destroyer; Death, the shatterer of worlds.'"

"And?" Chiun asked, his face hopeful.

"And what?"

"There is more?"

"'The dead night tiger made whole by the Master of Sinanju,'" Remo said.

Chiun relaxed. "You could not complete the prophecy the other night."

"What other night? Why, the night in the burning house, Remo. What did you think we were talking about?"

"In times past, when you heard that voice in your head, it was the shadow of Shiva taking hold of your mind, warning you, preparing you, calling you to preserve your body, for it is the vessel of the Destroyer. Now, Shiva had many incarnations. At times he is Shiva Mahedeva—Shiva the Supreme Lord. And other times as Shiva Bhairava—Shiva the Destroyer. In those times when you heard the voice speaking to you, or through you, you had become Shiva Remo."

"Sounds like a fifties song. Shivaremo doowop doowop."

"Do not jest. This is one of the sacred mysteries of Sinanju. Now, I have always thought the day would come when you would become Shiva Remo for good, and take my place as the next Master of Sinanju. But in that night, with your throat blue and your face smeared with ashes as Shiva's face is portrayed in the histories, you spoke against me, Remo. You were not Remo. Your voice was not Remo's. You were not Shiva Remo. You were Shiva Mahedeva, and you knew me not. Less did you care for me, who have made you whole."

"I'm sorry for the words I spoke, Little Father. But I do not remember them."

"I forgive you, Remo, for in truth you were not yourself. But I am worried. When Shiva is ready, he will take possession of your fleshly envelope. I do not want him to take over your mind too."

"But if that is my destiny, what can I do?"

"You must fight, Remo. You must assert yourself. You must remember Sinanju, and your responsibilities. Above all, you must continue my line."

Remo got to his feet and stood with his face to the wall.

"I don't want to lose you, Little Father," he said, his voice trembling.

"Become the next Master of Sinanju, and I will be with you always," Chiun said sadly. "This is my vow to you."

"I don't want to lose myself, either. I don't want to

be anything except Remo Williams. That's who I am. That's all I know."

"You have been chosen by destiny. It is not for us to rail against the cosmos, but you have a choice before you, Remo Williams, my son. You must make it soon. For soon, I may be gone. And at any time the terrible god of the Hindus may return to claim you as his own. And you will be lost forever."

9

Colonel Viktor Ditko knew he was near Sinanju when the stink of dead fish filled his nostrils.

He hastily rolled up the window of his Russian-made Chaika automobile.

"We are nearly there," Ditko called over his shoulder.

In the back, on the floor, Sammy Kee huddled under a rug.

"I know," said Sammy Kee. "I can smell it too."

"Is it always this bad?"

"No. It's actually worse when the wind is from the east. The smog."

Colonel Ditko nodded. For the last hour he had driven through some of the most heavily industrialized landscape he had ever imagined. Great smokestacks belched noxious fumes. Everywhere he looked there were factories and fish-processing plants. Once, they had driven over a rude iron bridge and the sluggish river below was a livid pink from chemical wastes. He saw few residential areas. He wondered where all the dronelike workers who must toil in the endless factories lived. Perhaps they slept at work. More likely, they slept on the job. It would not have surprised Colonel Ditko, who held a low opinion of Orientals in general and the North Koreans in particular.

Ditko followed the macadam road until it petered out into a dirt pathway that actually made for smoother driving, so bad had been the potholes in the paved road—which was alleged to be a main highway.

Suddenly the land opened up. The factories ceased to dominate the landscape. But curiously there were no houses, no huts, no signs of habitation. Before, peasants could be seen riding their ubiquitous bicycles down the road. No longer. It was as if the land that lay at the end of the road was poisoned. Ditko shivered at the eeriness of it.

When he ran out of road, Ditko drew the car to a stop next to a crude signpost of wood on which was burned a Korean ideograph that looked like the word "IF" drawn between two parallel lines.

"I think we are lost," he said doubtfully. "The road stops here. There is nothing beyond but rocks and an abandoned village."

Sammy Kee slid up from the protective depths of the rear seat. He blinked his eyes in the dull light.

"That's it."

"What?"

"Sinanju," said Sammy Kee, watching for North Korean police.

"Are you serious? This is a security area. Where is the barbed wire, the walls, the guards?"

"There aren't any."

"None? How do they protect their village, these Sinanjuers? And their treasure?"

"By reputation. Everyone knows about the Master of Sinanju. No one dares to approach Sinanju."

"Fear? That is their wall?"

"The old man in the village explained it to me,"

said Sammy Kee. "You can climb over walls, dig under them, go around them, even blow them apart. But if the wall is in your mind, it is infinitely harder to bring down."

Colonel Ditko nodded. "I will let you out here."

"Can't you escort me to the village? What if I get picked up by the North Korean police?"

"I will watch you until you enter the village, but I will not go any closer."

Colonel Ditko watched Sammy Kee slip out the back seat and pick his careful way from boulder to rock until he had passed from sight, down into the village of Sinanju. In his peasant clothes, the American was as much a part of North Korea as his fear-haunted face. Sammy Kee would be safe from the North Korean police, Ditko knew. They would not dare pass beyond the wall.

Colonel Viktor Ditko was certain of this, for he could see the wall himself, as clearly as if it were built of mortar and brick.

The first thing Sammy Kee did was to find the spot where he had buried his video equipment. The flat rock he'd used for a marker was still there. Sammy dug into the wet sand with his bare hands, the coldness numbing them, until he uncovered the blue waterproof vinyl bag. He pulled it free and undid the drawstring neck.

The video equipment—camera, recorder, belt battery pack, and spare cassettes—was intact. Sammy quickly donned the battery pack and hooked it up. He shivered, but it was still early. He hoped the sun would come out to warm his body.

Sammy climbed an outcropping of rock, feeling the rip and scrape of the brown conelike barnacles which were like the eyes of certain lizards. He had a perfect view of the village of Sinanju. There were the houses, mostly of wood and sitting on short wood stilts, and scattered on the ground like many thrown dice. In the center was a great open space, called the village square, although it was just a flat pancake of dirt. And facing the square, the splendid treasure house of Sinanju, the only building with windows of true glass and a granite foundation. It was the oldest structure, and it looked it, but even its carved and lacquered walls gave no hint of the great secrets those walls contained.

Sammy brought the video camera to his shoulder, sighted through the viewfinder, and filmed a ten-second establishing shot. He rewound the tape and played it back through the viewfinder. The equipment functioned perfectly. He was ready to begin.

As Sammy watched, the sleepy village came to life.

Cooking fires were lit and a communal breakfast began in the square. But something was different. The villagers were not dressed in their faded cotton, but in glorious silks and furs. Sammy watched for the old man who had talked to him so much of Sinanju—the caretaker, Pullyang. He would wait until Pullyang was alone and he would approach him. The old man knew everything there was to know about Sinanju. Perhaps he could force him to open the treasure house.

When Pullyang finally emerged, from, of all places, the treasure house itself, Sammy Kee was surprised. But his surprise turned to shock when, on a litter of sorts, a very old man was carried out into the plaza to the adulation of the crowd.

Walking beside the litter, tall and erect and proud in a way unlike the subservient villagers, was a white man. He wore Western-style clothes, slacks and a high-necked shirt.

And Sammy Kee knew with a sickness in the pit of

his empty stomach that the Master of Sinanju had returned to the village.

Sammy half-slipped, half-fell from the boulder. He landed on his rump, wondering what he should do. He dared not attempt to enter the treasure house now. That would be impossible. Not to mention fatal.

Escape, too, was impossible. Only one road led away from the sheltered cove that was Sinanju. And Colonel Viktor Ditko, as they had agreed, sat in his car, awaiting Sammy's return.

Sammy crawled on his hands and knees down toward the water. He did not know why he did that. He was frightened. He was sick of being frightened, but he had to do something—anything.

A teenage boy crouched down near the water, washing something. Sammy thought he must be a fisherman, cleaning his nets, but then he remembered the legends of Sinanju. Nobody fished in Sinanju. Not to eat, at least.

When the boy stood up, Sammy saw that he was not wetting a fishing net, but cleaning a stain from a great costume. A blue-and-green dragon. Sammy knew it was a dragon because the head lay beside a rock.

The boy, satisfied that the stain was gone, began to slip into the costume.

It was then that Sammy Kee understood what he had to do. After all, whose life was important?

He sneaked up behind the boy and struck him on the head with a rock.

The boy folded like a paper puppet. Quickly Sammy stripped the lax form of his costume, which was of colored rice paper and silk. It was full, voluminous, and would fit him with room to spare so that his battery pack belt was not obvious.

Sammy pulled on the silken folds. No one would recognize him in this. He shouldered the camera, and, balancing carefully, pulled the stiff paper dragon mask over his head.

The camera fit. The lens pointed down the open snout, and Sammy tested the angle of field. The camera, roving around, saw without obstruction. By accident, the crushed skull of the boy came into the viewfinder.

The boy was dead. Sammy hadn't meant to kill him. But it was too late for regrets. He was just another peasant anyway. Sammy Kee was a journalist.

Sammy paused to drag the boy's body into the cold sea before he trudged into the village of Sinanju, his head light with excitement, but his stomach heavy with fear.

Remo wasn't hungry, but that didn't stop him from taking offense.

The villagers of Sinanju were squatting all over the plaza, dipping their ladles into bowls of steaming soup and yanking gobs of meat off a roasted pig. In the center, the Master of Sinanju sat on his low throne, eating rice, the caretaker, Pullyang, beside him.

Remo sat downwind. Like Chiun's, his body was purified, he could not eat red meat or processed food. Or drink anything stronger than mineral water. So the smell of roasted pig offended his nostrils.

But it was the behavior of the villagers which offended Remo more. Here he was, the next Master of Sinanju—if Chiun had his way—the future sustainer of the village, and no one offered him so much as a bowl of white rice. Instead, they treated him like an idiot child the family only let out of the attic on special occasions.

Remo was disgusted. He had never understood why Chiun continued to support his lazy, ungrateful fellow villagers. They did nothing but eat and breed.

And complain. If they were Americans, they would all have been on welfare.

Remo laughed to himself to think that Sinanju had pioneered the concept of welfare. But so it seemed to him. He couldn't imagine living in Sinanju permanently, or taking one of the flat-faced, broad-hipped Sinanju women for a wife.

He wondered if he had a choice anymore.

"Remo, to me," Chiun called suddenly. Breakfast was over.

Remo walked through the squatting villagers. No one bothered to move aside for him.

"Remo, my son," Chiun whispered in English. "Help an old man to stand. But do not be obvious about it."

"Yes, Little Father," Remo said respectfully. He took Chiun by the arm and carefully helped him to his feet, making it look like Remo simply moved the throne aside in a gesture of courtesy. Chiun seemed smaller, slower, and Remo fought back a wave of emotion.

"Stand by my side now," Chiun said.

Remo stood. A sea of Korean faces looked up at him. They were as blank and expressionless as apple dumplings.

The Master of Sinanju shook his arms free of his flowing black sleeves, and raised them to draw attention to himself.

"My children," he intoned, "great is my joy, for I have at last come home. But deep is my sorrow, for my days as your Master are drawing to a close."

And at that a low hush fell upon the crowd. Remo saw tears appear on some faces. He wondered if they were for Chiun or because their meal ticket was fading before their eyes.

"Despair not, my children," Chiun continued, his voice lifting. "For I have not returned empty-handed. I have brought gold. I have increased our treasure manyfold. Lo, richer than ever is the House of Sinanju—thanks to Chiun."

And a cheer came up from the crowd. Some villagers, dressed in ornamental costumes, danced in joy. There, Remo saw a leaping heron, here a furry bear, representing Tangun, progenitor of the Korean race. Out from the rocks a man dressed as a dragon came running clumsily. He, too, joined in the dance, although his movements were awkward and less fluid than those of the others.

"Know that the Master of Sinanju suffered greatly in the land of the round-eyed whites," proclaimed Chiun, and Remo thought his voice, as he waxed flowery, also grew more vital. "In America, I served not the emperor, for America has no emperor, no king, not even a lowly prince."

The villagers gasped. It was an unbelievable thing.

"These Americans have, instead of a king or proper ruler, a thing called a president, who is not of royal blood. No, this ruler is chosen by lottery, as is his co-ruler, a thing called a Vice-President, who is well-named for he rules over a land of vice and license. Truly, this land has fallen into decline since the days when it was a colony of the good King George."

"You're laying it on too thick, Chiun," cautioned Remo.

"But I did not serve this President of America," continued Chiun. "No. I served a pretender, a physician known as Dr. Harold Smith, who claimed to be one of the most powerful men in America. Yet when the Master of Sinanju offered to dispose of the President of America and seat the pretender Smith on the throne of America, Smith would have none of it. Instead, this lunatic preferred to run an asylum for the mad, called by the meaningless name of Folcroft, while sending the Master of Sinanju hither and yon slaying the enemies of America."

"Is it true so, O Master?" asked a villager.

Chiun nodded solemnly. "It is truly so. Ask my adopted son, Remo, who is an American."

No one spoke up. It was as if Remo weren't there.

In Korean, Remo tried to explain.

"In America, we elect a new President every four years. It is our way. We are a nation of laws. But some evil people in America have bent the laws of my country to their own ends. Something had to be done. So a President years ago created a thing called CURE and put Dr. Smith in charge. It was Smith's job to fight the bad elements in America, and the enemies of my country throughout the world. He didn't want to rule America, just to protect it."

The women giggled.

"Tell about the Constitution, Remo," Chiun said in English. "They will find that amusing."

"It's not funny," Remo growled. But he continued speaking to the crowd. "In America, each man's rights are protected by a shield. It is called . . ." Remo turned to Chiun, and in English, asked, "How do you say 'Constitution' in Korean, Little Father?"

"Drivel," said Chiun placidly.

"It is called the Protector of Rights," said Remo, improvising in Korean.

Here the villagers leaned forward, for they understood shields.

"This shield was a document, on which all the rights of men were written. It says that all men are created equal and—"

Remo's words were drowned by gales of laughter.

"All men are created equal," the villagers chortled. "Not all Koreans are equal, but even the lowest are more equal than pale Americans."

"How can a paper shield protect a man? Does it not wear out being passed from man to man?" the caretaker, Pullyang, demanded.

"Because Americans believe in this shield," Remo answered.

"Americans must believe all shields are equal too," Pullyang said smugly. And the villagers howled.

Chiun silenced his people with his palms held out.

"That's better," Remo growled. "Years ago, a President of the United States saw that evil men were abusing the Constitution to make mischief. But the President could not fight these men without offending the Constitution."

"Why did he not tear it up?" asked a young boy.

"The Constitution is sacred to Americans," Remo shot back. "The same way the legends of Sinanju are sacred to all of you."

And that the villagers understood. They fell silent again.

"So this President created a secret organization called CURE to work around the Constitution, so it would not perish."

"He spat on the shield of his country?" asked someone.

"No, he didn't spit on it," Remo barked. "He worked around it."

"He pretended it did not exist?"

"No, he violated its laws so that he would not break faith with the American people."

"Why not make his own Constitution? Was he not the ruler?"

"He did not have the power. He was the protector of the Constitution, like . . . like a shepherd."

"America must be a land of sheep, then," scoffed Pullyang. "Their rulers are powerless and their people unthinking."

"No, that's not it!" Remo was getting angry. Why didn't these people try to understand?

Chiun touched Remo's shoulder. "I will finish your explanation," he said. "But it was a good try."

Remo frowned, stepping aside.

"Now, it is not the way of America to recognize an assassin," Chiun intoned. "They do not believe in assassins, but they needed one. So a functionary from America was sent to me. He would not hire an assassin, he said stubbornly. But he wished the services of Sinanju in training an assassin of their own. A Master of Sinanju would not do, this functionary, who was named MacCleary, insisted. This assassin must be white, because he would work in secret. He must be able to walk among whites unseen.

"And I said to this MacCleary that a Master of Sinanju is of more value standing beside a throne. When your enemies know you have employed the House of Sinanju, they will shrink from wickedness. Secrecy is for thieves. But this MacCleary would not, or could not, understand. How could he? He was white and from a land that had never employed a Master of Sinanju, for America was only two hundred years old. The white MacCleary insisted upon secrecy, and I told him that the color of an assassin is not what guarantees secrecy, but his skill. Still this MacCleary insisted. He said that the assassin they wished me to train would be charged with finding his own victims."

And the villagers of Sinanju laughed at the ridiculous logic of the Americans.

"And I told him it was the duty of the emperor to select the victim, the assassin's to execute him. It is an old understanding. The king does not kill and the assassin does not rule.

"Times were hard then. There had been no work. Some of you remember those days. There was talk of sending the babies home to the sea. So I took, to my great shame, this odious task. I agreed to train a white assassin for America—first extracting an agreement that America's assassin would not take work away from any future Master."

The villagers nodded their approval.

"Instead of a babe, they presented a man for me to train in Sinanju," Chiun said mockingly.

Laughter.

"And instead of a Korean, they gave me a white."

More laughter.

"But lo," said Chiun, his voice growing serious, "this white, although an eater of meat, was sound of limb. This white, although big of nose and clumsy of gait, was good of heart. And I taught him the first steps toward correctness. Grateful was this white. And he said to the Master, "I am but a lowly white, but if you will give me more Sinanju, I will follow you to the ends of the earth like a puppy dog, and I will sing your praises, O awesome magnificence.""

"Not bloody likely," Remo grumbled.

Chiun gently nudged Remo in the ribs with an elbow.

"And I said to this white, this sub-Korean, I said, 'I will do so because I have signed a contract, and contracts are sacred to Sinanju. Now the contract I signed was wondrous. No Master of the history of Sinanju had ever signed such a wondrous contract. This contract stipulated that I train this white in Sinanju, which I did, and it further stipulated that if this white's service was unsatisfactory, if he failed his white leaders, or if he shamed the House of Sinanju with incorrect posture or bad breathing or any similar great offense, the Master of Sinanju had the duty and obligation to dispose of this white like so much duck droppings."

Everyone looked at Remo.

"What else would you do with a recalcitrant white?" Chiun said, and beamed as a signal to the villagers to laugh. And they did.

Remo fumed.

Chiun grew serious again.

"But as the months passed while I trained this white, I discovered a remarkable thing." Chiun paused for maximum dramatic effect. "This white accepted Sinanju. Not merely in his flabby muscles or in his pale skin or in his dull mind, but in his heart. And it was then I knew that, while his skin was inferior, and his habits poor, his heart was Korean."

A few villagers made a show of spitting on the ground when they heard that.

"His heart was Korean," Chiun repeated. "A miracle! After all these years without an heir for the Master of Sinanju, I dared to hope that I had found a worthy successor. I trained him and trained him, lo these many years, breeding in Sinanju, and erasing the filthy white habits of the land of his birth, until the proper hour. That hour has now come. I present him to you, my adopted son, Remo."

The faces of the villagers of Sinanju regarded Remo with stony silence. Remo fidgeted.

"Tell them," Chiun hissed.

"Tell them what?"

"Of our decision. Quickly, while the crowd is with me."

Remo stepped forward.

"I am proud to be Sinanju," Remo said simply.

Stone silence.

"I am grateful for everything Chiun has given me."

Nothing.

"I love him."

The faces of some of the women softened, but those of the men grew harder.

Remo hesitated.

Chiun grabbed at his heart. "I hear nothing," he said under his breath. "It must be that I am failing."

"And I want you to know that I am prepared to assume the responsibilities as the next Master of Sinanju," Remo said suddenly.

The villagers cheered wildly. They stamped their feet. They danced. Those in costumes cavorted around Remo like he was the maypole. The dragon dancer kept getting in Remo's face.

"This is crap," Remo said angrily. "They hated me until I promised to support them."

"They were merely waiting for you to prove your Koreanness," Chiun said. "And now you have. I am proud."

"Hogwash," said Remo, and stormed off.

Chiun called but Remo did not respond. He kept walking, and the look in his eyes caused the crowd to part. All except the dragon dancer, who followed him at a careful distance, not really dancing, but certainly not walking normally.

Chiun slipped to the ground, taking again to his throne.

"What is this?" asked the caretaker, Pullyang.

"It is nothing," said Chiun. "He has looked forward to this great moment all his life. He is merely overcome with emotion." But Chiun's eyes were pained. "Perhaps we will postpone the great investment ceremony a few days," he said doubtfully.

10

Remo struck out to the north, not noticing where he was going. He just wanted to get away.

For the last few months Remo had been haunted by the need to find out who his parents were, and why they had abandoned him as a baby. It meant, really, discovering who he actually was. It had all seemed so important. But now that Chiun was dying and Remo faced the ultimate test of where his loyalties lay—with America or with Sinanju—it wasn't relevant any more.

What would happen, Remo wondered, when Smith didn't hear from him? Would he assume Remo was hurt, or killed? Would he send the U.S. Marines in to find out? Or would Smith even care, now that CURE operations were winding down?

But CURE operations never wound down. Remo knew Smith had been deceiving himself. This was just a lull. Soon, some crisis would rear its ugly head, and it would be back to business as usual. When the call came to return to America, what would he do? Remo wondered.

Remo looked back from a low hill. Sinanju lay below, with its tarpaper and wood shacks, pagoda-roofed houses, wooden sidewalks, and the magnificent treasure house. It looked like an Oriental's version of a Wild West town, and nothing like home. Not Remo's. Not Chiun's. Not anyone's.

Remo felt suddenly very, very tired. He had walked off to be alone with his thoughts and his frustrations, but now all he wanted to do was find some nice warm place—indoors—where he could nap.

Remo found such a place almost immediately.

It was a modest house by itself in a little vale, far from any other houses. By American standards, it was just down the road from Sinanju proper, but by the tightly knit standards of Chiun's village, the house was an outpost.

There were no signs of habitation as Remo approached. No bowl of radishes drying outside, no strings of noodles hanging in the sun. Maybe the occupant had died. Remo couldn't remember having seen the house in any of his previous visits to Sinanju.

He decided that if no one wanted it, he would take it.

Remo pushed the door in. It was unfastened.

Only a little light entered with Remo. It was very dark inside. That was good. He would sleep better in the darkness.

Remo's foot touched a floor mat. He lay down on it, starting to relax almost as soon as his spine felt the hardness of the floor under it.

"Maybe I'll wake up back home," Remo said wishfully.

"Who is it?" a small voice asked in the darkness. The voice spoke in Korean.

Remo shot to his feet. His eyes dilated automatically. Someone else was in the house, sitting in the darkness of one corner, sitting without light or sound.

"Hello?" Remo asked, embarrassed.

"I do not recognize your voice," the voice said. "Is there something that you want?"

The voice was light, lilting—a woman's voice.

"I thought no one lived here," Remo said. "I'm sorry."

"Do not be," the voice said sadly. "No one visits me."

"Why do you sit in the dark?"

"I am Mah-Li," the voice said. "By Sinanju law, I must abide in the darkness, so that no one will be offended by my ugliness."

"Oh," said Remo. He could see her, a shadowy figure in a yellow high-waisted dress. Her traditional Korean bodice was white and airy. One hand covered her face protectively while the other reached into a pocket and extracted something filmy. When she took both hands from her face, she was wearing a heavy gauze veil behind which liquid eyes glinted. He felt sorry for the girl. She must be deformed.

"I am sorry to disturb you, Mah-Li," Remo said in a small voice. "I was looking for a place to rest." He started for the door.

"No," Mah-Li called, reaching out. "Do not go just yet. I hear celebration in the village. Tell me, what transpires?"

"The Master of Sinanju has come home."

"This is welcome news. Too long has he dwelt in far places."

"But he is dying," said Remo.

"Even the mightiest tide ebbs," Mah-Li said softly. "But the flowing back to the sea is a sad thing nonetheless." Remo could tell she was deeply affected. It was the first hint of true feelings anyone in Sinanju had expressed about Chiun.

"You are sorry?" Remo asked.

"The Master of Sinanju is a candle that has illuminated the world since before the days of the great warrior king Onjo, who built the first castle in Korea," Man-Li said thoughtfully. "It is a shame that he dies without heir. It will break his heart."

"I am his heir," said Remo.

"You? But your voice is strange. You are not of Sinanju."

"Not of the village," said Remo. "But I am Sinanju. Chiun has made me Sinanju."

"It is good," said Mah-Li. "The traditions must be kept. Some of them, anyway." And she touched her veil self-consciously.

"You live alone?" Remo asked.

"My parents died before I had memory. I have no one. The men will not have me because of my ugliness. They called me Mah-Li, the beast."

"You have a lovely voice," Remo said, not sure what else to say. By American standards, the ordinary women of the village were unhandsome. He wondered how much worse Mah-Li was. Maybe she was like the Elephant Man, all covered with knobs and tumors.

"Thank you," Mah-Li said simply. "It is good to talk to someone who has a kind heart."

Remo grunted. "I know what you mean. Chiun's people aren't high on compassion."

"They are what they are."

"I'm an orphan too," Remo suddenly blurted out. He wasn't sure why he said it. It just popped out of his mouth.

"It is a terrible thing, to be alone."

Remo nodded. A silence passed in the room. Remo felt like a teenager at his first high-school dance, uncertain of what to say or do next.

"Would you like tea?" Mah-Li asked shyly.

"Tea would be fine," said Remo.

Mah-Li got to her feet. Remo saw that she was short, like all Sinanju woman, but not so stocky. Most of the woman of Sinanju were built like Eskimos. Mah-Li was slim and delicately boned. Her natural scent wafted to Remo's nostrils and he found it surprisingly pleasant.

There was a little charcoal stove on the floor in one corner, typical of Korean homes. Mah-Li got a cooking fire going with some flint and wood shavings.

Remo watched her delicate movements in silence. He saw grace and poise, and whatever Mah-Li's face must look like, her form was as supple as the willow tree.

When the water was boiled, she poured it into a blue-green ceramic tea server and set two matching cups without handles—like those Remo had seen in many Chinese restaurants, except that these were wonderfully ornate—and set them before him.

"Very pretty," Remo said.

"They are celadon," Mah-Li said. "Very precious. The server is carved in the shape of a turtle, which to us symbolizes long life."

"Huh? Oh, the tea," Remo said, flustered.

"Of course. What did you mean?"

Remo said nothing. He hadn't meant the tea service. He wasn't exactly sure what he meant. The words had just come.

Mah-Li poured the tea and handed one cup to Remo. Her slim fingers lightly brushed Remo's outstretched hand, and he felt a tingle that ran up his arm and made his toes curl involuntarily.

There was something intoxicating about being in her presence. Intoxicating, but somehow soothing. The inside of the house was mellow in the light of the stove. It threw shadows that made Remo think of safety and security.

Was Mah-Li some kind of Korean witch? Remo thought suddenly.

"Drink," said Mah-Li.

"Oh, right." Remo took a sip, and watched surreptitiously as Mah-Li bent forward so that she could drink without Remo seeing her veiled face. But her eyes caught the light, and Remo was suddenly overcome by an intense curiosity to see behind that tantalizing veil.

Impulsively he leaned forward, his hands ready to pull the gauze free.

Mah-Li, sensing Remo's intent, stiffened, but curiously, she did not move to block Remo's hands.

There came a knock at the door.

The windows were shuttered. It was impossible to see inside.

Sammy Kee searched for some chink in the walls, and found none.

He had gotten some of what he'd returned to Sinanju for. A videotaped confession of the Master of Sinanju's service in America, and a nearly complete account of the workings of a secret arm of the United States government, known as CURE. For a moment, Sammy Kee's half-forgotten journalistic instinct had taken over. It was the story of the century. Any television network would pay a small fortune for it.

And so Sammy Kee had quietly followed the American named Remo after he'd stormed away from the town square of Sinanju. If only he could get more. Who was this Remo? What was his last name? How had he come to be chosen to be the next Master of Sinanju?

Sammy wondered if he knocked on the door and asked to borrow a cup of rice, could he get Remo to talk directly to the camera, maybe trick him into an interview without Remo realizing it.

No, too risky. He had to get this new tape back to Colonel Ditko. Maybe it would be enough to satisfy him. And he was afraid to linger much longer. But Sammy was also a journalist, and to him, the story was everything.

But hours passed, and Remo did not reappear.

What was he doing in there? Sammy Kee wondered. Colonel Ditko was waiting for him back along the road. He was almost certain he had enough footage. But what if Ditko sent him back for more? And there was the body of the boy whose skull Sammy had crushed with a stone. What if someone missed the boy?

Crouching in the rocks, the chill winds of the Yellow Sea cutting through the paper of his costume, Sammy Kee grew impatient.

And so, he made a terrible mistake.

He knocked on the plain wood door.

Remo answered it. He took one look at the dragon dancer and said, "Tell Chiun I'll see him later."

Sammy asked, "Can you spare some rice?" in Korean. He pressed the trigger of the video camera.

"Rice?" Remo looked puzzled. "I don't—"

Remo's hand drifted out so suddenly that Sammy Kee didn't notice it. His dragon head went sailing into the air. Looking into the viewfinder, Sammy only saw Remo's face. It twisted in anger.

"What the ding-dong hell?" Remo yelled, lapsing into English.

Sammy Kee felt the videocam leave his hands. The electrical cable drawing the power from his belt battery pack snapped. Sammy's hands were suddenly numb. He looked at them. They were stuck in the stricture of holding the camera. But the camera wasn't there.

"Who the hell are you?" Remo demanded.

"Don't hurt me! I can explain," Sammy babbled in English.

Remo grabbed Sammy by the shoulder, tearing off the top of the beautiful dragon costume. Underneath, he saw Sammy's dirty peasant clothes.

"You're an American," Remo said accusingly.

"How did you know?" Sammy asked.

You smell like an American. Everyone smells like something. Koreans smell of fish. Americans smell of hamburger."

"I admit it. Don't hurt me!"

"Smith send you?"

"What?"

"Smith," Remo repeated angrily. "He sent you, right? You're here to spy for him, to make sure I come back to the States after . . . after . . ."

Remo didn't complete the sentence. The very thought of Smith sending a spy all the way to Sinanju to monitor Chiun's dying was too much, even for a cold-blooded tightass like Smith.

"Come on," Remo said, yanking Sammy Kee along.

"Where are you taking me?" Sammy wanted to know.

"Don't talk. Don't say a word. Just walk."

Sammy looked back in the shadows of the open door, a small figure stood in a forlorn posture, her face concealed by a impenetrable veil. She waved farewell timidly, but Remo didn't notice the gesture. His eyes were on the road ahead. The beach road leading back to the village.

The Master of Sinanju was troubled. He had tricked Remo into declaring himself as his true heir. But at what cost? Remo had been very angry. It made Chiun heavy of heart. And so Chiun had retired to his beautiful house, deciding in his mind that he would not go to Remo, but would instead wait for Remo to seek him out.

And if the Master of Sinanju expired before Remo's anger had subsided, then that would be on the head of Remo Williams.

Pullyang, the caretaker, entered upon knocking.

"He returns, O Master," Pullyang said as he bowed.

"His face?" asked Chiun.

"Full of wrath."

Chiun looked stricken, but he said, "I will meet with him."

"He is not alone. One is with him."

"Which?" asked Chiun. "Speak his name."

"I am told this person is not of the village."

"This too, I will deal with." And Chiun was puzzled.

Remo barged in without knocking. Chiun was not surprised. But he was surprised when Remo threw down a Korean whom Chiun did not recognize.

"If this is a peace offering, Remo," Chiun said, "it will not do. I have never seen this wretch before."

"Forgive me, great Master of Sinanju," pleaded Sammy Kee, falling to his knees.

"But I will consider your offering," added Chiun, who enjoyed proper respect.

"Smell him," Remo said.

Chiun sniffed delicately.

"He smells of excrement," the Master of Sinanju said disdainfully. "And worse, the dreaded hamburger."

"A present from Smith," Remo said, holding up the video camera. "He was spying on us."

Chiun nodded. "Emperor Smith is concerned that the line of succession is being transferred correctly. The mark of a wise ruler. I would not have credited him so. Too bad his contract is with the current Master of Sinanju, and not the next one."

Chiun addressed Sammy Kee.

"Return to your homeland and inform Emperor Smith that the Master of Sinanju lives yet. And that Remo will not be returning, having agreed to take my place as the head of my village."

Sammy Kee trembled in silence.

"But," Chiun went on, "if he should wish to employ the next Master on a nonexclusive basis, this could be discussed. But the days of Sinanju having only one client are over. Sinanju is returning to its honored tradition of employment, which you Americans have only lately discovered. I believe you call it diversification."

"What'll we do with him?" Remo asked. "There's no submarine in the harbor. I checked."

"Hold him until the vessel reveals itself."

"I found something else in the harbor, Chiun."

"Your manners?" asked Chiun.

"No. A body. Some kid."

Chiun's wispy facial hair trembled.

"A drowned child," he said sadly.

"His head was bashed in. The crabs got him."

Chiun's hazel eyes turned to Sammy Kee. They blazed.

And the fear Sammy Kee felt deep inside him sweated out of his pores and proclaimed to the sensitive nostrils of the Master of Sinanju, better than any admission by word and deed, the undeniable guilt of Sammy Kee.

"To murder one of Sinanju is an unforgivable crime," said Chiun in a low voice. "But to murder a child is abomination."

Chiun clapped his hands twice to signal. The sound hurt Sammy's eardrums and set the wall hangings to fluttering.

The caretaker, Pullyang, entered, and seeing Sammy Kee, recognized him. But he said nothing.

"Find a place for this wretch. He will be sentenced at my leisure. And send men to the harbor to claim the body of the poor child that lies there."

Sammy Kee tried to bolt from the room.

"Not so fast, child-killer," Remo said. He tripped Sammy Kee with the toe of one Italian loafer. Sammy crashed to the floor and Remo touched his spine down near the small of the back.

Sammy Kee suddenly discovered that his legs

wouldn't work. He tried to crawl, but his lower body was so much dead weight. He cried.

"What will happen to him?" Remo asked casually.

"The crabs in the harbor have eaten sweet today. Tomorrow they will eat sour," Chiun said.

"Smith won't like it."

"Smith is a memory to the House of Sinanju from this day forward. You have renounced him."

"I'm not sure I've renounced anything, Little Father. Just because I agreed to support this place doesn't mean I can't work for Smith."

"You are a cruel child, Remo."

"How do you feel?" Remo asked in a softer tone.

"The pain is less when you are with me," he said.

"Can we talk later?"

"Why not now?"

"I have something to do," said Remo. He seemed strangely eager to leave.

"Something more important than comforting an old man?"

"Maybe."

Chiun turned his face away. "You will do what you will do, regardless of the hurt you cause."

"I still have to think this through," Remo said.

"No," Chiun shot back. "You have yet to think. The day you think is the day you feel compassion. I have decided not to move from this spot until that day arrives."

And when Remo didn't answer, Chiun looked back.

But Remo was gone.

Chiun gasped at the blatant lack of respect. His brow furrowed. It was beyond understanding. Remo had not appeared angry with him, but he clearly was not responding to Chiun's blandishments.

Chiun wondered if Shiva were stirring in Remo's mind again.

11

Colonel Viktor Ditko waited outside the invisible wall surrounding Sinanju until night fell.

Cold crept into the darkened interior of his Chaika. It made his right eye ache beneath his new eyepatch. The doctors had repaired the ruptured cornea, but it would be weeks until Colonel Ditko would know if the eye was any longer good.

Colonel Ditko shivered in his winter uniform, cursing the name of Sammy Kee under his breath. He dared not turn the heater on and use up all his gasoline. Gasoline was not easily come by in North Korea, where automobiles were for the privileged only, and gas stations nonexistent. Colonel Ditko couldn't afford to seek out an official gas depot, where there would be questions about his presence here, far from his post in Pyongyang.

Colonel Ditko wondered if Sammy Kee had escaped. But Sammy Kee would not have done any such foolish thing. There was no escape in North Korea. Only through Colonel Ditko could Sammy Kee ever hope to escape North Korea. So, watching the full moon rise above the low hills, Colonel Ditko shivered and settled deeper into the cushions, wait-

ing for Sammy Kee to come up to the road from
Sinanju.

But Sammy Kee did not come up the road from
Sinanju. No one came up the road from Sinanju. It
was as if Sinanju had gobbled up Sammy Kee like a
hungry bear.

The night had nearly elapsed when Colonel Ditko
came to the only possible conclusion left to him.

Sammy Kee had been captured or killed in Sinanju.

Colonel Ditko had tasted failure before in his career. Failure, it might be said, was a hallmark of
Colonel Ditko's KGB career. It was the only hallmark, according to his superiors, which was why
they frequently transferred him from one career-
crushing post to another. Colonel Ditko could live
with failure. Ordinarily.

But not this time. This time he had sacrificed an
eye to ensure success. This time he had promised
success to the General Secretary himself. He could
admit failure to his immediate superiors—they expected no better from him—but not to the General
Secretary. He would have him shot. Worse, he might
be exiled to the worst possible KGB post in the
world. Back to India, this time to stay.

This time, Colonel Viktor Ditko decided, stepping
from the half-warmth of his closed car, he would not
settle for failure.

He walked down the road toward Sinanju, the
moonlight making an excellent target of his slight
form, and his Tokarev handgun clenched tightly in
one hand. It was the hardest walk Ditko ever under-
took, because to get into Sinanju, he had to walk
through a wall. Even if he couldn't feel it.

Sammy Kee lay in the darkness of the hut where
they had thrown him. It was not so bad now. Before,

the door was left open and the villagers paraded past to see the child-killer. Sometimes they spit upon him. Some came in and kicked him until blood climbed up his throat.

The worst moment was the woman though. She was a fury. She was young, but with the seamed young-old face of the childbearing women of Korea. She screamed invective at Sammy Kee. She spat on his face. Then she flew at him with her long-nailed claws. But the others dragged her back just in time, before she could rake his face to peelings.

Sammy understood that she was the boy's mother and he felt sick all over again.

With the coming of night, they locked the door and left Sammy with the horror of his situation. He could move his arms, but his legs were useless. There was no feeling below his waist. He massaged his dead legs in a vain effort to restore circulation and nerve feeling, but all that happened was that his bladder gave and he soaked his cotton trousers.

Finally, Sammy gave up trying to restore his legs. He dragged himself to the videocam which they had tossed in like a piece of junk, and laid his head on it, using the rubber handle as a kind of pillow. He was desperate for sleep.

The fools, Sammy thought, the greatest journalist of the century and they had treated him like a dead cat. And then the peace of sleep took him.

Sammy awoke from his slumber without knowing why.

The door opened cautiously. Moonlight shimmered off a pair of eyeglasses, turning the lenses into blind milky orbs.

Sammy recognized the slight unathletic form.

"Colonel Ditko," Sammy breathed.

"Quiet!" Ditko hissed. He shut the door behind

him and knelt down in the darkness. "What has happened?"

"They caught me," Sammy said breathlessly. "They're going to kill me. You must help me escape."

"You failed?" Ditko said hoarsely.

"No, no! I didn't fail. Here. I made a new tape. It contains everything."

Colonel Ditko scooped up the videocam.

"Play it back through the viewfinder," Sammy said eagerly. "You'll see."

Ditko did as he was bidden. In his eagerness, he placed the viewfinder to his right eye. Annoyed, he switched to his good eye. He ran the tape, which played back minus sound.

"What am I seeing?" Ditko asked.

"The Master of Sinanju. He has returned. And he brought with him the American agent he has trained in Sinanju. They tell everything. They are assassins for America. It's all on that tape."

Colonel Ditko felt a wave of relief.

"You have succeeded."

"Help me now."

"Come then. We will leave before light."

"You must help me. I can't move my legs."

"What is wrong with them?"

"The one called Remo. The Master's American pupil. He did something to them. I have no feeling in my legs. But you can carry me."

Colonel Ditko unloaded the tape from the videocam.

"I cannot carry this and you."

"But you can't leave me here. They'll kill me horribly."

"And I will kill you mercifully," said Colonel Ditko, who placed the muzzle of his Tokarev pistol into Sammy Kee's open mouth, deep into his mouth, and pulled the trigger once.

Sammy Kee's mouth swallowed the sound of the shot. And the bullet.

Sammy Kee's head slipped off the barrel of the gun with macabre slowness and struck the floor in several melonlike sections.

Colonel Ditko wiped the backsplatter blood from his hand on Sammy's peasant blouse.

"Good-bye, Sammy Kee," said Colonel Viktor Ditko. "I will remember you when I am warm and prosperous in Moscow."

And Viktor Ditko slipped back into the night. This time he knew the walk through the invisible wall would not be that difficult.

The caretaker, Pullyang, brought the word to the Master of Sinanju with the chill of the Sinanju dawn.

"The prisoner is dead," he said.

"Fear of the wrath of Sinanju extracts its own price," said Chiun wisely.

"His head lies in pieces."

"The mother," said Chiun. "She cannot be blamed for seeking revenge."

"No rock ever burst a skull in this fashion," Pullyang insisted.

"Speak your mind," said Chiun.

"A western weapon did this," said Pullyang. "A gun."

"Who would dare profane the sanctity of Sinanju with a shooter of pellets?" demanded Chiun.

Pullyang said nothing. He lowered his head.

"You have something else to tell me."

"Forgive me, Master of Sinanju, for I have committed a grave trespass."

"I cannot forgive what I do not understand."

"This American was here before. A week ago. He asked many questions, and I, being proud of my

village, told him many stories of the magnificence of
Sinanju."

"Advertising pays," said Chiun. "There is no fault
in that."

"This American carried a machine with him, the
same one he had yesterday. He pointed it at me
when I spoke."

"Fetch this machine."

When Pullyang returned, he offered the videocam
to the Master of Sinanju, who took it in hand as if it
were an unclean fetish.

"The receptacle for words and pictures is missing,'" Chiun said. "It was not missing last night."

"It is so, Master of Sinanju."

Chiun's eyes lowered as he thought. A man had
recorded the words of the caretaker Pullyang one
week ago. Now he had returned to record more of
the same. But this time, he had recorded the Master
of Sinanju and his pupil, for Chiun knew that the
dragon dancer at yesterday's breakfast feast was
Sammy Kee.

What did this mean? Chiun did not fear for Sinanju.
Sinanju was inviolate. The dogs of Pyongyang, from
the lowliest to the Leader for Life, Kim Il Sung, had
made a pact with Sinanju. There would be no trouble from them.

The mad Emperor Smith was not behind this.
Chiun did not always understand Smith, but Smith's
mania for secrecy was the one constant of his de-
ranged white mind. Smith would not dispatch persons to record the secrets of Sinanju.

Enemies of Smith perhaps, seeking gain. Or enemies of America. There were many of those. Even
America's friends were but slumbering enemies, pre-
senting a smiling visage but clutching daggers behind their backs.

Presently Chiun's eyes refocused.

"I forgive you, Pullyang, for in truth you are, compared to me, young, and unwise in the ways of the outer world."

"What does this mean?" asked Pullyang gratefully.

"Where is Remo?" asked Chiun suddenly.

"He has not been seen."

"By no one?"

"Some say he walked toward the house of the beast."

"Go to the house of Mah-Li the unfortunate and fetch my adopted son to me. I do not understand what transpired last night, but I know that it must concern my son. Only he can advise me in this matter."

"Yes, Master of Sinanju." And Pullyang, greatly relieved that no blame was attached to him, hied away from the house of the Master, who suddenly sank into his seat and closed his eyes with a great weariness.

The tape cassette arrived from Pyongyang by diplomatic pouch. In the pouch was a note from the Soviet ambassador to the People's Republic of Korea demanding to know why the head of embassy security, Colonel Ditko, was sending packages directly to the Kremlin through the ambassador's pouch.

As he loaded the cassette into his private machine, the General Secretary made a mental note to inform the Soviet ambassador to mind his own business regarding the activities of the People's Hero, Colonel Ditko.

The General Secretary watched the tape to the end. He saw an old man and a Caucasian exhorting a crowd of peasant Koreans. According to the note from Colonel Ditko, the tape showed the legendary Master of Sinanju and his American running dog confessing to espionage, genocide, and other crimes against the international community on behalf of a renegade United States government agency known as CURE.

There was a crude transcript with the tape, and an apology from Colonel Ditko, who explained that his Korean was not good, and that for security reasons he had not had the tape translated by someone more fluent. And by the way, the Korean-American, Sammy Kee, had met an unfortunate death in the course of making this tape.

The General Secretary called the supreme commander of the KGB.

"Look through the non-persons list and find me someone who speaks fluent Korean," he ordered. "Bring him to me."

Within the day, they had exactly the right person, a dissident history teacher who specialized in Oriental studies.

The General Secretary ordered him locked in a room with only a videotape machine, pen and paper, and instructions to translate the cassette tape from Korea.

By day's end, the transcript was delivered, sealed, to the office of the General Secretary.

"What shall we do with the translator?" asked the courier.

"He is still locked in the viewing room?"

"*Da.*"

"When the smell of death seeps into the corridor, in a week or two, you may remove the body."

The courier left swiftly, his kindly opinion of the worldly new General Secretary forever shattered.

The General Secretary read the transcript through once, quickly. And then again, to absorb all the details. And a third time to savor the sweetness of this greatest of intelligence coups.

A smile spread over the open features of the General Secretary, making him look like someone's well-fed and content grandfather.

It was all there. The United States had a secret agency known as CURE, one unknown even to the Congress of the United States. It was illegal, and indulged in assassinations both in America and abroad. The assassins were trained in Sinanju. In theory, they could go anywhere, do anything, and never be suspected.

And then the General Secretary remembered stories that had circulated in the upper levels of the Politburo before he had assumed his current rank. Fragmentary rumors. Operations that had been stopped by unknown agents, presumably American. Strange accidents that defied explanation. The liquidation of Soviet *Treska* killer teams during the time when America's intelligence services had been emasculated. The strangeness during the Moscow Olympics. The failure of the *Volga*, a space device that would have become the ultimate terror weapon had not unidentified American agents neutralized it. The disappearance of Field Marshal Zemyatin during the ozone-shield crisis two years ago.

In a locked cabinet in this very office, the General Secretary had a file of KGB reports of those mysterious incidents. The file was marked "FAILURES: UNKNOWN CAUSE."

But now the General Secretary knew the cause was no longer unknown. It could be explained in one word: CURE.

The General Secretary laughed to himself. Privately, he admired the boldness of the American apparatus. It was brilliant. Exactly what America needed to deal with her internal problems. He wished he could steal it.

But that wasn't the way the General Secretary did business. His predecessors would have tried to steal

it. Not him. He would simply ask for it. No harm in
that, thought the General Secretary. And he laughed.

He picked up the red telephone which connected
directly to the White House and which he was reserved to use only in times of extreme international
crisis. This would wake up the President of the United
States, the General Secretary thought, as he listened
to the tinny feedback ring from Washington. And he
laughed again.

12

Remo Williams wondered if he was falling in love.

He barely knew the maiden Mah-Li. Yet, even with Chiun weakening daily, Remo was drawn back to the house of the girl the village of Sinanju had ostracized as the beast, like a poor sailor who had heard the siren call of Circe.

Remo could not explain the attraction. Was it the mystery of her veil? Fascination with the unknown? Or was it just that she was an understanding voice in a troubled time? He did not know.

It bothered Remo terribly that Chiun, in his last days, continued to carp and try to lay guilt on him. Remo wanted to be with Chiun, but Chiun was making it impossible to be around. And, of course, Remo felt guilty about that, too.

So Remo sat on the floor of Mah-Li's house, telling her everything, and wondering why the words kept coming out. He usually didn't like to talk about himself.

"Chiun thinks I'm ignoring him," Remo said, accepting a plate of a Korean delicacy that Mah-Li had baked just for him. It smelled good in the darkened room.

"What is this?" he asked, starting to taste a piece.

"Dog," said Mah-Li pleasantly.

Remo put it down abruptly. "I don't eat meat," he said.

"It is not meat," laughed Mah-Li. "Dog is rice bread, filled with dates, chestnuts, and red beans."

"Oh," said Remo. He tried it. "It's good."

"Aren't you?" asked Mah-Li.

"What?"

"Ignoring the Master?"

"I don't know. I'm all confused. I don't know how to deal with his dying. I've killed more people than I can count but I've never lost anyone really close to me. I've never *had* anyone really close to me. Except Chiun."

"You do not wish to face the inevitable."

"Yeah. I guess that's it."

"Ignoring the dying one will not keep him breathing. He will die without you. Perhaps sooner."

"He seemed okay when I talked to him. It's so hard. He doesn't look like he's dying. Just tired, like he's a clock that's winding down."

"Will you go back to your country when it is over?" Mah-Li asked. Remo realized she had the knack for saying just enough to keep him talking.

"I want to. But I promised Chiun I'd support the village, and I'm not sure what I would be returning to. Chiun has been my whole life. I see that now. Not CURE, not Smith. And I don't want to lose him."

"It can be pleasant living in Sinanju. You will take a wife and have many children."

"I don't want any of the village girls," Remo said vehemently.

"But you cannot marry a white girl," said Mah-Li.

"Why not? I'm white. Although Chiun doesn't think so."

No? What does the Master think?" she asked.

"That I'm part Korean. It's crazy. With one breath he castigates me as a clumsy white. With the other he tries to convince me of my Korean heritage. According to him, somewhere in the line of Sinanju, there's an ancestor of mine. Isn't that crazy?"

Mah-Li looked at Remo through her veil and he studied her. Mah-Li's face was a pale oval behind the gauze but he could not discern her features. He felt drawn to look, even though it made him uncomfortable.

"I think there is a little of Korea in your face, around the eyes. Their shape, but not their color. The people of my village do not have brown eyes."

"Chiun just wants to justify giving Sinanju to a white man," Remo said.

"Have you ever heard the story of the lost Master of Sinanju, Remo?" Mah-Li asked quietly.

Remo liked the way Mah-Li pronounced his name. She had to force the R and she rolled it in the Spanish style.

"Lost Master? Was that Lu?"

"No, that was another Master."

"You know the story?"

"Everyone knows the story," said Mah-Li. "It was many years ago. There was a Master who was known as Nonga, whose wife bore him many daughters, but sadly no sons. Many were the daughters of Nonga, and each year another was born. And Master Nonga grew sullen, for he was unable to sire a male heir. By law, Sinanju could only be passed through the male line."

"Another strike against this place," said Remo.

"One year, when Master Nonga was very old, his wife, who was not so old, finally bore him a son. And the Master named this son Kojing, and he was very proud. But his wife kept a secret from Nonga, for she had in truth borne him two sons, as identical as snow peas. She hid the other son, whom she named Kojong, for she feared that the Master would slay Kojong, for there was a law in Sinanju that only the firstborn could be taught Sinanju. And Kojing and Kojong were born at the same time. She feared the Master Nonga, to solve this dilemma would drown one son in the cold waters of the bay."

"How did she keep the second one hidden?" asked Remo. "This isn't a big place, even now."

"She was very clever, this wife of Master Nonga. She hid the babe in the hut of a sister during Kojong's baby years. And when Kojong was a boy, he was in all ways identical to Kojing, and so she enlisted Kojing and Kojong in a game. On even days Kojing would live with Master Nonga and be his son, eating with the family and knowing parents, and on the other days, Kojong would live in the hut, and pretend to be Kojing. And this went on until the two boys were two men."

"You mean the old guy never caught on?"

"He was very old, and his eyesight, although excellent for seeing far things, was not good for things near. Master Nonga did not suspect he had two sons. When the time came to teach Kojing Sinanju, the trickery continued. Kojing learned the first day's lesson and at night taught it to Kojong, who took the lesson of the second day and passed it on to his brother, and so this went until both had absorbed Sinanju.

"On the day Kojing was invested as the next Master, Master Nonga died, for in truth he lived only as long as he needed to fulfill his obligations, for he was very tired of baby-making and being the father of so many useless girls."

"I bet," Remo said.

"And on that day, Kojong revealed himself. But there could be only one Master of Sinanju, and so

Kojong, because he was not Kojing, the boy Master Nonga thought he was training alone, announced that he was leaving Sinanju, and leaving Korea, to live. He pledged not to pass along knowledge of the sun source, but instead to pass along only the spirit of his ancestors, the many Masters of Sinanju, saying to the village, 'The day may come when a Master will sire no sons and the line of Sinanju will face extinction. On that day seek out the sons of Kojong, and in them find a worthy vessel to carry on the traditions.' And so Kojong sailed into the cold mists of the bay."

"Did any Master of Sinanju ever turn to an ancestor of Kojong?" Remo asked.

"No one knows."

"Chiun never told me that story."

"It is the way of the Master to do what he does. We do not question it here."

"Maybe I'm descended from Kojong."

"If so, Kojong's spirit has at last returned to Sinanju," she said.

"Yeah, but I'm not carrying the spirit of Kojong inside me, according to Chiun. I'm carrying the spirit of Shiva."

"In Sinanju, we believe that we have lived many lives. The spirit does not change, just the color of the eyes that the spirit sees with."

"Before, sometimes I've known things," Remo said. "It's like I'm carrying memories of Sinanju inside of me, memories of Masters who have gone before. I never understood it before. But the way you just explained it to me, "I think I understand now."

"You belong here, Remo."

"I do, don't I?"

"It is your destiny. You should accept it."

"I could live here, Mah-Li. If you would share this life with me," Remo said.

Mah-Li turned away. "I cannot."

"Why not?"

"It is forbidden."

"I am the next Master of Sinanju," Remo said with conviction. "I decide what's forbidden around here."

Impulsively Remo leaned forward and with both hands lifted the veil from the hidden face of Mah-Li, the beast.

Remo, who had seen many strange things in his life, was unprepared for the sight which greeted his eyes.

He gasped.

For Mah-Li was beautiful. Her face was intelligent and animated, her skin smooth as poured cream. Hair as black as a raven's wing framed the delicate beauty of her beautifully modeled features like a setting for the work of a master artisan. Laughter lurked well back in her eyes, as if waiting to be released, but it was there. Her eyes were Western eyes, like Remo's, not slanted, and he laughed aloud as he realized that was why the villagers called her ugly.

"Maybe I'll stay here," Remo said suddenly. "Maybe you'll marry me?"

"It is for the Master of Sinanju to give his approval of what you ask."

"Then I'm going to see him—right now," Remo said, jumping to his feet.

Remo ran into the caretaker, Pullyang, on the way to Chiun's house.

"The Master wishes your presence," Pullyang said.

"I'm on my way."

Chiun was sitting on his throne in the treasure house of Sinanju when Remo entered. The Master of Sinanju looked like an old turtle, slowly lifting his head at Remo's approach.

"Are you surprised to find me still among the living?" Chiun asked, seeing the shocked expression on his pupil's face.

"You look awful," Remo said. "How do you feel?"

"Betrayed."

"I had to be by myself," Remo said defensively.

"Then why were you with the one known as Mah-Li, if you had to be by yourself?" Chiun asked.

"Don't be a grouch," Remo said, taking a lotus position before the Master of Sinanju. "You never told me about her."

Chiun shrugged. "I have news."

"So have I. I've decided. I'm staying."

"Of course. You pledged yourself before the entire village."

"You're welcome," Remo said sarcastically. "Don't make this more difficult than it is, okay?"

"I am listening," Chiun said.

"I won't wear a kimono."

"The investment kimono has been handed down the line since before Wang the Greater," Chiun said slowly. But his eyes grew brighter.

"Okay. Maybe then. But not after."

"Done," said Chiun.

"And I won't grow my fingernails long."

"If you wish to deprive yourself of the proper tools with which to ply an assassin's trade, who am I to correct you? You are beyond correction."

"But I *will* choose a Sinanju girl."

Chiun perked up in his seat. He beamed. He took Remo's hand in his two yellow claws.

"Speak her name. I know it will be music to my aged ears."

"Mah-Li."

Chiun dropped Remo's hand as if it were a gutted fish.

"She is not appropriate," he snapped.

"Why not? I love her."

"You do not know her."

"I know enough to know I love her. And why didn't you tell me about her before? She's gorgeous."

"What do you know of beauty? Have you ever listened to one of my Ung poems without leaving in the middle?"

"Six-hour recitals about bees and butterflies don't do it for me, Little Father. And what's wrong with Mah-Li?"

"She is ugly. She will bear ugly children. The Master of Sinanju who will come from your seed must one day represent us in the outside world. I will not have my house shamed by hideous emissaries."

"That reminds me. Whose idea was it for her to go veiled? Yours?"

"The women of the village decreed it, so that she would not frighten the children or the dogs."

"Monkey spit," Remo snapped. "They were jealous of her."

"Your whiteness blinds you to the truth," Chiun retorted. "Name me one positive quality she possesses."

"She's kind. I can talk to her."

"That is two. I asked for only one. Besides, if you wish conversation and kindness, I have both in full measure."

"Don't duck the issue. Maybe I love her. Maybe I should marry her."

"You have loved unwisely before. You got over those ones. You will forget this one. I will send her away, if that will help you."

"I want Mah-Li. But she won't have me without your permission. Dammit, Chiun, I'm giving you what you want. Give me something in return. Give me one good reason I can't be with her."

"She is without family."

"And I have sixteen brothers and sisters? We already know it's going to be a small wedding party."

"She has no dowry."

"So?"

"In Sinanju, no maiden may enter into marriage without offering something to the father of the groom. Custom demands that the father of the bride provide this tribute. But Mah-Li has no family. No dowry. No marriage. These rules were made before our great-great-great-grand-ancestors. They are inviolate."

Remo jumped to his feet angrily.

"Oh, great. Because of some horseshit tradition, I can't marry whoever I want? Is that it? Is that what you're telling me, Chiun?"

"Tradition is the foundation of our house, of our art."

"You just want the freaking tribute. Isn't that it? You don't have enough gold in this place already?"

Chiun looked shocked.

"Remo," he squeaked. "There is no such thing as too much gold. Have I not drummed that into your head?"

"Into my head, but not into my heart. I want to marry Mah-Li. You want me as the next Master. That's my price. Take it or leave it."

"We will speak of it another time," said Chiun, changing the subject. "I have already postponed the investment ceremony. Perhaps you are not ready yet."

"That's your answer?"

"No. That is my thought. I will think more on this matter, but there is first another, more pressing."

"Not to me," said Remo. "And why didn't you tell me the story about Kojing and Kojong before this?"

"Where did you hear the tale?" demanded Chiun.

"Mah-Li told me."

"I was saving that tale for the investment ceremony. And now she has ruined the surprise. Another reason not to marry her. She is a carrier of tales. They make inferior wives."

"No Mah-Li, no Master of Sinanju. You think about it," Remo said, and walked toward the door.

Chiun called out: "The spy you caught is dead."

Remo stopped. "So?"

"I did not kill him. Someone with a gun entered the village last night and butchered him."

"Why is it butchery when someone uses a gun? Dead is dead, isn't it?"

"Remo!" Chiun said, shocked. "Sinanju does not slaughter. Sinanju releases one from life. Is there no end to your insolence?"

Remo shut up.

"Better," said Chiun. "The one who invaded Sinanju took with him the cassette from this recording machine."

"What was on it?"

"Who knows? You. Me. All of us. Our words. Our secrets. Emperor Smith's secrets."

"You think someone's going to make trouble?"

"I hear a breeze in the distance," said Chiun.

Remo cocked his ear to the door. "Sounds quiet to me."

"This is not a breeze that blows through the air, but one which blows through the lives of men. It is just a breeze now, but soon it will gather force and become a wind, and as a wind it will grow bolder still, and it will be a typhoon. We must be ready for this typhoon, Remo."

"I'm ready for anything," Remo said, rotating his thick wrists impatiently.

Chiun shook his head sadly. Remo was obviously not ready at all. And there was so little time left. Chiun felt the weight of the future of Sinanju—a future that might now be smoke—on his frail shoulders.

13

No history book would ever record the superpower summit in Helsinki, the capital of Finland. No one knew it took place, except for the President of the United States and the General Secretary of the Soviet Union, and only a handful of very trusted aides. And of the group only the two world leaders knew what was discussed.

"A summit?" the President's chief of staff said. "Tomorrow?"

The President had just gotten off the hot line. The Soviet General Secretary had called unexpectedly, offering to meet secretly on a matter of critical international concern.

The President had accepted. He had not wanted to, but he knew from the brief conversation that he had no choice.

"I'm going," the President said firmly.

"Impossible, sir," the chief of staff stated. "We have no preparation time."

"We're going," the President repeated.

The chief of staff saw the cold anger in the President's eye. "Very well, Mr. President. If you'll kindly inform me of the agenda of matters to be discussed."

"That's classified," was the tight-lipped reply.

The chief of staff almost choked on the jelly bean the President had handed him.

"Classified? I'm chief of staff. Nothing is classified from me."

"Now you know different. Let's get going on this."

"Yes, Mr. President," the chief of staff said, wondering how the President was going to hold a meeting with the Russian leader so that no one, including the press, knew about it.

He found out that afternoon when the President's personal press secretary announced that the President was, on the advice of his doctor, taking a week's vacation at his California ranch.

The White House press corps immediately descended upon the topic of the President's health. Instead of issuing the usual denials, the press secretary gave a tight-lipped "No comment."

The press secretary walked away from the White House briefing room trying to conceal a satisfied smile. By tonight, the White House press corps would be encamped outside the perimeter fence of the President's California compound, trying to shoot telephoto pictures through the windows, which, if they hadn't been the press and the President a public figure, would have gotten them all arrested on Peeping Tom charges.

When *Air Force One* left Andrews Air Force Base that evening, it vectored west as the network cameras recorded its takeoff. What the cameras did not record was *Air Force One* setting down in a small military air base and suffering a hasty makeup job. The presidential seal was painted over, and the plane's serial numbers changed. A quick application of enamel spray paint changed the aircraft's patriotic trim.

When *Air Force One* was again airborne, it was a

cargo plane. It flew east, out over the Atlantic on a heading for Scandinavia.

In Soviet Russia, no such subterfuge was required. The General Secretary ordered his official TU-134 aircraft readied for a flight to Geneva. His aides were not informed of the reasons. There didn't have to be any.

The next morning, the Soviet plane descended on the airport in Helsinki. The freshly painted cargo plane carrying the President of the United States was already sitting on a runway that was closed, ostensibly for repairs.

The Soviet General Secretary sent a representative to the disguised *Air Force One*. The President at first refused an invitation to board the Soviet plane.

"Let him come to me," the President said through his chief of staff.

But the Soviet leader was insistent. As leader of a great power, he could not be expected to enter a lowly cargo plane of dubious registry, even in secret.

"They have us there," the chief of staff groaned.

"Very well," the President said. "I'm on my way."

"We're on our way," the chief of staff corrected.

The President fixed his chief of staff with a baleful glare. "You stay here and make fresh coffee. Strong. Black. I have a feeling I'm going to need it when this is over."

The Soviet General Secretary greeted the United States President in a soundproof cabin in the rear of his personal jet.

They shook hands formally and sat. The cabin smelled of the Russian's musky cologne. There was a small TV and video machine on a tabletop. The President noticed it subconsciously, no idea of its critical importance touching his thoughts.

"I am pleased you could meet me on such short

notice," the General Secretary said. He smiled expansively. The President hated it when he smiled like that. It was the same shit-eating grin he had flashed at Iceland.

"What's on your mind?" the President asked. He was in no mood for small talk, even if this was the first time the two leaders had met since the Russian, in his continuing quest to appear more Western, had gone to the trouble to learn English.

The General Secretary shrugged as if to say: I just want to keep this friendly. But he said: "I will get to the point. As I hinted over the phone, I know all about CURE."

"Cure?" the President asked, trying to sound calm. "The cure for what?"

"I mean CURE, as in all capital letters, CURE. The secret American agency whose existence demonstrates that the U.S. Constitution is a sham, a piece of political fiction."

The President knew it was all over, but he decided to play the hand out.

"Knowledge is not proof," he said pointedly.

"No," the General Secretary admitted, tapping the Play switch on the video recorder. "But proof is proof. Allow me to entertain you with this. It was filmed in the People's Democratic Republic of Korea." And when the President looked perplexed, he added: "*North* Korea. More specifically, in the modest fishing village known as Sinanju. I believe you have heard of it." There was that grin again.

The video screen came to life. And there was the Master of Sinanju. The President recognized him. Chiun had personally guarded the oval office during a recent threat to the President's life. It was impossible to forget Chiun.

Chiun spoke in Korean, and at first the President was relieved. No matter what secrets Chiun spilled in

Korean, they would have less impact shown over U.S. television, even with subtitles.

But then an American appeared beside Chiun. The President knew he must be Remo, CURE's enforcement arm. As Chiun spoke to a crowd of villagers, Remo interposed comments, some in Korean, but others in English. Remo had to ask Chiun for the proper Korean words for "Constitution."

"Here is a complete transcript of what they are saying."

The President took it wordlessly and glanced at the first few pages. It was all there. America's greatest security secret, and it had been handed to him by the Soviet General Secretary.

"We know all about it," said the General Secretary. "About Master Chiun, Remo, and Emperor Smith."

"If you call him emperor, you can't know it all."

"We know enough."

And the President agreed. Looking up from the transcript, he had deep pain in his eyes.

"What do you want?"

"It is simple. It is fair. For more than a decade, America has had a secret weapon to handle its domestic affairs."

"That is our right," the President bristled.

"I will not disagree with you. The question of the illegalities of this enforcement arm of yours is your political problem. We in Russia have had similar arrangements in the past, our KGB, and before that the Cheka. But my country is concerned over the use of this CURE apparatus in international affairs."

"Specifically?"

"Specifically, we do not know. We have no proof yet that your CURE has operated on our soil. But there have been many strange incidents among agents of our foreign service. Projects mysteriously abandoned. Agents killed in odd ways. Others who disappeared. We have never been able to account for these failures. I will not ask you about them now. Most took place prior to my regime, and they belong to the past."

"What do you want?" the President repeated.

"Before I place my demands before you, let me point out to you that you have been employing an agent—I refer to the illustrious Master of Sinanju—who comes from our sphere of influence. You have made numerous secret submarine landings—according to this tape and another in our possession—in North Korean waters. Communist waters."

"No comment."

"Good. You understand the political damage of that revelation alone and apart from the business of CURE. Then understand I am only asking for what rightfully belongs to Mother Russia."

"Belongs—!"

"We want the Master of Sinanju. We want CURE erased from existence. And we want this Remo person."

"So you can meddle in international affairs? This is blackmail."

"No. We merely want an advantage that America has enjoyed in secret for many years. Now it is Russia's turn."

"Blackmail."

"Such a harsh word. I prefer to call it parity."

"Remo is a patriot. He won't work for you. And I can't turn him over to you. That would be a deed more politically damaging than if the world sees that tape."

The Premier considered.

"Abandon CURE. Give us the Master of Sinanju. And let us negotiate with this Remo. If he turns us down, what would you do with him?"

"Remo would have to die."

"So let it be that way. Our mutual problem is solved."

"I can't turn CURE over to you. It would be a knife at America's throat."

"I understand your fear. Let me quell it. I do not want the Master of Sinanju to enforce our political will in your hemisphere. I wish to use him as you have, to make our system of government work in spite of its flaws. Crime is growing in Russia. Drunkenness, laxity in the work force. These are Russia's deepest ills. You know that I have been trying to solve them."

"Yes, I know."

"Then you can sympathize with my plight. The plight of Mother Russia. We want a dose of your CURE, too."

The President's mind worked furiously. He wished he had his advisers here now. But if he did, they would have to die after advising him. He was all alone in this one.

Finally he said, "I'm damned if I do and damned if I don't."

"Not exactly. If you'd like I could draw up a treaty assuring you that Russia would not employ the Master of Sinanju outside of the so-called Soviet bloc for a grace period of, say twenty-five years. Surely that is a greater period than the lifespan of the current Master of Sinanju."

"Who would draw up the treaty? You? Me? We can't trust anyone else with the knowledge."

"I see your point," the General Secretary said. "Then let us trust to a handshake."

"I have no choice," the President said stiffly, rising to his feet. "I will issue the directive to disband CURE immediately. Give me a day to work out the details. The rest is up to you."

The General Secretary shook the President's hand warmly, and grinned.

"And our representative will approach the Master of Sinanju about new employment. As they say in your country, it is a pleasure doing business with you."

The President mumbled something under his breath that the Russian leader took to be some informal acknowledgment, and he nodded even as he made a mental note to ask his official English tutor the meaning of the colloquial American phrase "Up yours."

In Rye, New York, Dr. Harold W. Smith was having an ordinary day. The sun shone through the big one-way windows. Outside it was pleasantly warm for this late in the fall and there were boaters on Long Island Sound.

His secretary, Eileen Mikulka, a bosomy middle-aged woman wearing bifocals, had just dropped off the preliminary budget sheets for Folcroft's next quarter.

"That will be all, Mrs. Mikulka," Smith said.

"Yes, Dr. Smith," Mrs. Mikulka said crisply. At the door, she turned to add, "Oh, I spoke with the electrical contractor this morning."

"Um-hum," Smith said absently, immersed in the budget forms.

"They'll be here tomorrow to look at the backup generator."

"Fine. Thank you."

"You're welcome, Dr. Smith," Mrs. Mikulka said, closing the door. She wondered if her employer had understood any of what she had said. That man could get so absorbed in his columns of figures. Well, she would remind him again tomorrow.

It was an ordinary day. Which in the life of Harold W. Smith meant an extraordinary day. His early-morning scan of incoming CURE-related data had revealed only updates of ongoing situations. No action was required on any of them. And so Dr. Harold W. Smith was spending his day actually working on Folcroft affairs—something he usually delegated to his secretary.

He did not expect the phone call from the President of the United States. And he did not expect this particular call.

Smith let the direct line to the White House ring several times before answering. He did not do this out of self-importance, but to emphasize the true nature of CURE's unwritten charter. The President who had originally set up CURE had been aware of the possibility of abuse of the enormous power of the organization. Not by Smith—who was considered too patriotic and, more important, too unimaginative to implement a power grab—but by a future President. Thus, Dr. Harold W. Smith was entirely autonomous. The President could not order CURE into action. He was limited to three options: imparting information on developing situations; suggesting specific missions; and—and here, the check-and-balance system reversed itself—he could order CURE to disband.

Dr. Harold W. Smith picked up the telephone on the fifth ring, assuming the President was calling to invoke one of the first two options.

"Yes, Mr. President," Smith said coolly. He never let himself become friendly with any of the Presidents under which he served. He refused to vote for the same reason.

"I'm sorry to have to do this, Dr. Smith," said the familiar garrulous tones, now strangely subdued.

"Mr. President?"

"I hereby direct you to disband your organization. Effective immediately."

"Mr. President," said Smith, betraying surprise in

spite of himself, "I know America is edging closer to no longer needing this organization, but don't you think this is precipitous?"

"I have no choice."

"Sir?"

"We've been compromised. The Soviets know all about us."

"I can assure you there's been no leak from this end," Smith said stiffly. It was typical of him that he thought first of his reputation, and not of the more personal consequences of the presidential order.

"I know. I have just met with the Soviet General Secretary. The bastard handed me a videotape of your people. They spilled their guts to the camera."

"Remo and Chiun? They're in Sinanju."

"According to what the transcript of the tapes says—and I don't dare verify it for obvious reasons—Remo has gone over to the other side."

"To the Russians? I can't believe that."

"No, not to the Russians. He's defected to North Korea. He's agreed to work for his teacher's village. It's on the damned tape."

"I see," said Smith. But he didn't see. Remo was an American. Had Chiun drummed Sinanju into him until he was no longer himself?

"The Soviets want them both. That's their price for silence."

"We can't give them Remo and Chiun."

"We can't not. As dangerous as those two are in the wrong hands, we can't admit that our system of government doesn't work. That's why your organization was started, isn't it?" The President's tone softened. "You did your job admirably, Smith, and I'm sorry. But we're going to cut our losses on this one."

"Remo would never agree to work with the Soviets. He's a patriot. That's one of the reasons he was selected for this."

"That's the Russian's problem. They want to negotiate with Chiun themselves. They want Remo dead. They want CURE disbanded."

"There's a problem with that," said Smith.

"There better not be," said the President hotly. "I'm giving you a direct order."

"The Master of Sinanju is in ill health. That's why he's gone back to Sinanju. Remo thinks he might be dying."

"Then the joke is on the Soviets. We may come out even on this one in the end."

"Some of us, Mr. President," Smith said.

"Uh, yes. Sorry, Smith. I didn't create this situation."

"I will leave for Sinanju immediately to terminate our contract with Sinanju."

"I'll inform the Soviets that they can go into Sinanju at sunset tomorrow. The rest will be up to them."

"Good-bye, Mr. President."

"Good-bye, Smith. I'm sorry it had to end in my administration. Your country may never know your name, but I will remember your service as long as I live."

"Thank you, Mr. President," said Dr. Harold W. Smith, and hung up the direct line to the White House for the final time. He upended the phone and, with a dime, unscrewed a plate to reveal a tiny switch. He pressed it. Instantly the phone went dead. There was no longer a line to Washington, nor any trace that one had ever existed. Just a telephone with no dial and melted circuitry.

Smith took a special briefcase from a locked cabinet and went into the outer office.

"I'm leaving early, Mrs. Mikulka," he said.

"Yes, Dr. Smith. Have a good day."

Smith hesitated.

"Dr. Smith?"

Smith cleared his throat. "Please file those budget

reports I left on my desk," he said hastily. And then he ducked out the door. He was never any good at good-byes.

Smith drove to his house, his briefcase open on the seat beside him. It contained a mini-computer, telephone hookup, and modem, which linked with the Folcroft computer net. Smith issued the orders that would set in motion the complicated relay of transportation necessary to get him to Sinanju. He wondered what it would be like. He had heard so many stories.

As he drove, Smith noticed the beauty of the turning leaves. The scarlets of the poplars, and yellows of the oaks, the burnt oranges of the maples. They were beautiful. Strange that he had not noticed them before. He instantly regretted that he would never look upon them again.

"Harold?" said Mrs. Smith, surprised to find her husband in the upstairs bedroom, packing. "I didn't know you were home."

Smith felt a pain stab at his heart. He had sneaked in, hoping to avoid his wife. He hadn't wanted to face saying good-bye to her, either. He was afraid it would cloud his resolve.

"I'm in a rush, dear. Late for an appointment." He did not look up from his packing.

Maude Smith saw the old familiar bulge of a shoulder holster under Harold Smith's gray jacket, and the tight, drawn look that her husband had worn so many years before. But seldom these days.

"Tell me Harold."

"Dear?"

"The gun. The look on your face. It's like the old days. Before Folcroft."

"An old habit," Smith said, patting the spot under

his armpit. "I always carry it during business trips. Muggers, you know."

Maude Smith sat on the neatly made bed and touched her husband's arm lightly.

"I know all about it, dear. You don't have to hide it from me."

And Smith swallowed the acid that rose in his throat.

"For how long?" he asked hoarsely, avoiding her eye, trying to finish packing. But his hands trembled.

"I don't know. I've always suspected it. A man like you doesn't retire from intelligence work. We went through too many years together for me not to know the signs."

Smith thought back to his OSS days, searching his mind for the most painless method of death he could administer.

"I never dreamed you knew," Smith said, looking stonily ahead.

"I didn't want you to worry about my knowing, silly."

"Of course not," Smith said hollowly.

"Don't look so pained, dear. I've never mentioned to anyone that you were still with the CIA."

"CIA?" asked Smith in a blank voice.

"Yes. Your retirement was a ruse, wasn't it?"

Smith rose from his packing. He sucked down a climbing sob. Tears of relief came, the first he could remember crying in decades.

"Yes, dear," said Dr. Harold W. Smith, grateful that he would not have to kill his wife to protect his country. "My retirement was a ruse. Congratulations on guessing the truth."

Maude Smith stood up and gave her husband a motherly peck on the cheek.

"Vickie called today. She's planning on coming for the weekend."

"How is she?" Smith asked.

"Just fine. She asks about you constantly."

"She's a wonderful daughter," Smith said, wishing he could see her one more time before he went.

"Will you be back in time?"

"I doubt it," Smith said quietly.

And Mrs. Smith read more into that quiet statement than her husband would have dreamed.

"Harold?" she asked tentatively.

"Yes?"

"Are you in a terrible rush?"

"Very."

"Can you spare just a few minutes for me? For us?"

And Smith saw that her chin trembled just as it had on their wedding night, so many years ago.

He took off his jacket and held her in his arms.

"I've always loved you," she said. "Every minute of every day."

He could only respond, "I know," and hold her tighter.

In San Diego, Captain Lee Enright Leahy was dining on pork chops and baked potatoes when a lieutenant strode into the base officers' mess and offered him a salute and a packet of sealed orders.

Captain Leahy thought he was having an attack of *déjà vu* when he read those orders in the privacy of his quarters. The orders were to prepare to return to Sinanju. Today.

Captain Leahy picked up the phone and did something that should have gotten him court-martialed. He called the admiral to protest top-secret orders.

The admiral said, "I have no idea what orders you are talking about."

"Thank you very much for your cooperation, sir!" barked Captain Lee Enright Leahy, sounding very much like an angry Annapolis cadet given extra cranking duty. He thought the admiral was observing proper protocol by denying knowledge of the orders he had signed.

What Captain Lee Enright Leahy did not know, and never suspected, was that the admiral really didn't know anything about the order to return to Sinanju. Or any previous Sinanju mission, although his signature had appeared on them all. He was as much in the dark as anyone.

Except Dr. Harold W. Smith, who had made it all happen.

14

Remo stopped between the Horns of Welcome, high over the rocky Sinanju beach. Down a shell-strewn path, he could see the simple shack of Mah-Li, and he sat on a damp flat rock to try to sort out his feelings.

He had known love before. In the days before Sinanju, he had loved a girl named Kathy Gilhooly. They had been engaged but Remo's arrest had ended that. There was Ruby Gonzales, whom Remo wasn't sure if he ever loved, but they had been friends. Ruby was the only other person ever to work for CURE and when she decided to quit the organization, she disappeared. And there had been Jilda, the Scandinavian warrior woman he had met when he was last in Sinanju, during the so-called Master's Trial. Remo's commitment to Sinanju had gotten in the way of their love and she had gone before Remo learned, too late, that she had been carrying his child. He wondered where she was now. Had the child been born? Was it a boy or a girl?

But Remo had never felt a pull like the one he felt toward Mah-Li. It was as if she were the other half of him, lost and unsuspected for all his life. Now that they had found each other, even in the turmoil he felt, she put him at ease.

It seemed that every time Remo had found someone important, he was cheated by fate. Now, it was happening again.

Remo stood on the beach with his hands in his pockets, wondering what to do.

He felt his wallet, dug it out. It contained a sheaf of bills, useless in Sinanju, some credit cards, a few fake identity cards supplied by Smith, all in different names. He looked through them. There was an FBI agent's card in the name of Remo Pelham, a private detective license in the name of Remo Greeley, and a fire marshal's card in the name of Remo Murray.

"Screw this," Remo said, sending the cards skipping, one by one, across the Bay of Sinanju. "From now on I'm just Remo Williams."

He tore the bills to pieces, shredded the leather wallet, and tossed it into the surging tide too.

There was a bunch of coins in the other pocket. Remo dug them out and started to pitch them across the waves one by one. Each coin flew farther than the others.

Remo was down to his last few pieces of change, thinking that with each toss he was ridding himself of another piece of his past, when he saw the conning tower push up from the surging surf. And the American flag painted on its side.

"Shit," said Remo, wondering if he should just disappear. But when he saw, across the miles, Dr. Harold W. Smith emerge topside and step into an inflating rubber raft, he instead sat down on a rock to wait for him.

Smith came alone. He wore the inevitable gray three-piece suit, and the even more inevitable briefcase lay at his knees. Salt spray wet them both. Remo grinned at the absurd sight.

Smith let the raft beach itself before stepping out. Remo went down to meet him.

"Remo," Smith said, as if they were coworkers bumping into one another in an office corridor.

"If you're here to take me back to America," Remo said, "you're too late. If you're here for the funeral, you're too early."

"Good. I must speak with Chiun. But first, I must ask you a question."

Shoot."

"Please answer truthfully. Would you consider working for the Soviets?"

"No way," said Remo.

"I'm glad you said that," said Smith, pulling his automatic.

Remo had sensed the movement even before Smith's brain had given the command to draw. Smith's arm was still in motion when the gun suddenly jumped into Remo's hand.

"Nice try, Smitty," Remo said. "But you know better."

"I had to try," said Smith unemotionally.

"You've disbanded the organization, am I right?" asked Remo, pulling the clip from the gun and throwing the components in opposite directions. "And you don't need me anymore."

"The President gave the order," Smith said. "The Russians have found out about CURE. We have to disband."

"Fine. Disband. Just do it someplace else. I've got things on my mind."

"I wish to speak with the Master of Sinanju."

"I don't think he wants to talk to you."

"I'm afraid I must insist."

"You have nerve, Smitty. First you try to kill me, then you want me to take you to Chiun, figuring you can get him to kill me."

"Will you take me to him?"

Remo grinned broadly. "Sure. My pleasure." And he dragged Smith all the way back to Sinanju, just fast enough that Smith had to run to keep his feet.

"Guess who came to dinner, Little Father," Remo said, when he entered the treasure house.

Chiun looked up from his scrolls with tired eyes.

He gave a tiny bow of his head. "Emperor Smith, your presence is welcome. You are here, of course, to witness the investment ceremony."

"No," said Smith, clinging to his briefcase. "Master of Sinanju, I must speak to you . . . alone."

"Forget it, Smitty. He won't kill me. I'm head of the village now."

Chiun stared at Smith with impassive eyes.

"I have no secrets from Remo. Although it cannot be said that he has no secrets from me."

"Very well, Master of Sinanju. First let me remind you of your contract with the United States, specifically clause thirty-three, paragraph one."

"I remember that clause," said Chiun. "A worthy clause. Perhaps outdated, but sufficient for its time."

"The cherry blossoms are in bloom," said Smith, giving the agreed-upon code word for Chiun to kill Remo. It had been part of their agreement.

"I am old and failing in vigor," said Chiun. "I do not believe I understood your words."

"I said, 'The cherry blossoms are in bloom,' " repeated Smith in a louder voice.

"Ah," said Chiun. "I understand now. You wish me to eliminate Remo, as per our agreement. Unfortunately, I cannot do that. Remo is about to become the reigning Master of Sinanju—"

"Maybe," added Remo. "If we can work out the details."

"—and it is forbidden for one Master to kill another," finished Chiun.

"But Remo isn't reigning Master yet," insisted Smith.

"True," said Chiun, his fingernails fluttering in the air. "But he has agreed to support my village. That makes him of my village, and Masters are forbidden to harm fellow villagers. I am sorry, but the Remo you gave me to train no longer exists. In his place stands this Remo, who is no longer the flabby meat-eater of our first meeting, but one in Sinanju. I cannot kill him."

"See?" Remo said smugly. "I told you."

"If there is someone else you would like me to kill, I will be glad to consider it," said Chiun.

"I see," said Smith. "Very well. I must tell you that the Russians have discovered my operation."

"Good for them," said Chiun, returning to his scrolls.

"The organization is to be disbanded. We've agreed to turn you and Remo over to the Soviets in return for their silence."

Chiun paused, and carefully placed his goose quill back in its inkstone.

"Masters of Sinanju are not slaves," he said gravely. "To be bartered like chattel."

"The Soviets will be here by sunset to take control of the village."

"You sold us out!" yelled Remo. "You sold me out! You sold my village out!"

And Chiun smiled at that last.

"We had no choice," Smith said imperturbably.

"We'll fight," said Remo.

Chiun held up a commanding hand.

"Hold!" he said. "Emperor Smith, am I to understand that you have sold our contract to the Russian bear?"

"Ah, I don't . . . If you put it that way, yes."

"The contract of the House of Smith," said Chiun solemnly, "binds my house to do your bidding. To do what you wish, there must be a formal signing over of the contract. Are you prepared to do this?"

"Yes," said Smith.

"Chiun, what are you saying? We can't work for the Russians."

"No," said Chiun. "You cannot work for the Russians. You must stay here and take my place. I must go to Russia and fulfill my last contract. It is my duty."

"I thought you said we were through with Smith."

"We are,'" said Chiun blandly. "Has not Emperor Smith himself just proclaimed it so?"

"That's right. I did," said Smith.

"You keep out of this," Remo snapped.

"But Emperor Smith's contract is still in force. I cannot die with an unfulfilled contract in my name. My ancestors, when I meet them in the Void, would shun me for eternity."

"I can't believe you're saying this, both of you," Remo cried.

Chiun clapped his hands imperiously.

"I grow weary. Leave me, both of you. We will assemble in the square when the Russians arrive. For now, I am an old man and I wish to enjoy in relative peace my final moments in the house of my ancestors."

"Come on, Smitty," Remo growled. And Remo yanked Smith out the door.

"Don't think badly of me, Remo," Smith said when they were outside. "We all understood it might come to this when we joined CURE."

"I didn't join, remember? I was hijacked."

"Uh, yes," said Smith uncomfortably.

"Things were bad enough until you came along," Remo complained. "Couldn't you let him die in peace?"

"You know the position I'm in," said Smith, dropping to his knees. He opened his briefcase. "You once believed in America."

"I still do," Remo said. "But things are different. I've found what I've been looking for here. What are you doing?"

"Taking care of unfinished business," said Smith, booting up the mini-computer. When the screen was illuminated, he keyed in a sequence of numbers and hooked the phone into the modem.

Remo watched as the words "ACCESS CODE REQUIRED" filled the screen.

In the space below, Smith typed the code word "IRMA."

The words "ACCESS DENIED" appeared on the screen.

"You goofed," said Remo. "You must be slipping."

"No," said Smith. "I deliberately used the wrong code. I just erased our secondary computer files on St. Martin."

"You're really going through with it," Remo said.

Smith keyed in another number sequence. Again the words "ACCESS CODE REQUIRED" appeared.

This time Smith typed in the name "MAUDE."

"ACCESS DENIED," the screen said.

"Folcroft?" asked Remo.

Smith stood up, locking the briefcase.

"I'm afraid so."

"Just like that?"

"Part of the safety system," said Smith. "In these days of tapping into computer records by phone, I had to come up with a fail-safe tamperproof system. CURE records can only be accessed by a code word. Anyone entering the wrong code word—any code word—would automatically throw the system off line. Just now I used the code words designated to erase the files permanently."

"Your wife's name and her nickname," said Remo.

"Wasn't that risky? Suppose someone else had used them?"

"That was the idea. It's common to use a wife's name as an access code. Anyone who knew those two names would obviously know about me. That kind of unauthorized knowledge by itself would signal that we were compromised, and file erasure would be just a prelude to disbanding."

"Well, that's that,'" said Remo.

"Not really," Smith said grimly. "I was supposed to be erased with them."

In Rye, New York, in the basement of Folcroft Sanitarium, the computer banks containing every particle of data belonging to CURE, the government agency that officially did not exist, and now no longer existed unofficially, received the microwaved transmission from Sinanju and initiated the code request sequence.

There was a pause while the access-code request was sent back to Sinanju. The computers hummed softly, awaiting the proper code word. Or the improper one, which would strip their memory banks of all data. File tapes twitched in quarter cycles. Lights blinked. The computers waited.

Then the lights went out.

"Oh my goodness," said Mrs. Mikulka, who was at her desk several floors above.

Then she remembered. The electrical contractor.

She took the stairs to the basement because the elevators were inoperable.

She found the contractor examining the backup generator in the dark with a flashlight.

"What happened?" Mrs. Mikulka demanded.

"Sorry about this, lady. I tried switching from the mains to this baby and—*boom*!—she blew. Completely. This is going to take a few days to fix now."

"Dr. Smith will be furious," said Mrs. Mikulka.

"Can't help it. This unit is pretty worn out. Can't figure out why. It's supposed to be for backup only. Am I right?"

"That's right."

"Well, you must have bought this baby used. It's worn down to nothing."

"Never mind," said Mrs. Mikulka. "What about our power? We have patients."

"No problem. Give me a minute to throw the circuit breakers on the mains."

Mrs. Mikulka felt her way back up the stairs, wondering what she would tell Dr. Smith when he returned.

Then the lights came back on.

Behind a concrete wall in the basement, not far from the faulty generator, a secret bank of computers resumed their operation, awaiting transmission of the CURE access code.

When, after several minutes, no signal was received, the computers resumed normal operations, searching nationwide data links for signs of potential criminal activity, as they had for over twenty years of continuous operation.

15

The Russians arrived exactly at sunset. Five Chaika automobiles led by a Zil limousine pulled to a halt at the edge of the village of Sinanju. The people of the village, seeing uniformed men bristling with weapons emerge from the cars, scattered to their huts in fear.

Remo saw the Russians coming down the rocks, one in KGB green, the rest in black uniforms like none he had ever seen before. He ran to the treasure house and burst in.

"Chiun. I'm not letting this happen," Remo said.

Chiun handed a freshly-rolled scroll to the caretaker, Pullyang, and waved for him to leave.

"You do not have to let anything happen, egotistical one," he said quietly. "It is happening without you."

"We'll fight them, Little Father."

Chiun shook his head wearily. "I cannot fight them."

"Then I'll do the fighting. There's only about a dozen of them. Piece of cake."

"Yes," said Chiun. "You could easily best the dozen. But what about the next dozen? And the two dozen who will show up at my village when the others do not return? And the legions who will surely follow. We are safe from the dogs at Pyongyang, but they are vassals to the Russian bear. The bear will keep coming until he has filled his stomach. No matter how many Russian corpses we pile in the village square to show our might, in the end my village will be lost." Chiun shook his head sadly. "No. This way is better."

"Bull!" said Remo.

"Once before, a Master of Sinanju was in service to an emperor, and when that emperor lost a war, his goods became the property of the conquering emperor. This calamity would not have happened had not the Master of that time, whose name was Tipi, been away at a crucial time. Have I told you that tale, Remo?"

"Screw the story. If I'm stuck in Sinanju, you're staying here, too."

"You have made up your mind?"

Remo folded his arms across his chest. "Definitely."

"Very well. Then bring me the sword of Sinanju. Quickly. Before the Russians are knocking at this door."

Remo took the sword, a two-handed weapon with jewel-encrusted hilt and a seven-foot blade, from its place of honor on one wall. He brought it to Chiun, offering it flat in his palms, blade turned inward.

"I do not wish to hold it," snapped Chiun. "It is for you. Now, quickly, strike off my head," and the Master of Sinanju bowed his head, giving Remo a clean opening to the back of his wattled neck.

"No," said Remo, horrified.

"Do it!" commanded the Master of Sinanju. "If you wish to spare me the pain of exile, then spare me the shame of willfully violating my sacred duty. And grant the Master who has made you whole a clean death."

"No!"

"Why do you hesitate, my son? With one stroke, you would cut yourself free of your obligations to me, and to my village."

Remo dropped the sword. He was in tears.

"You could return to the land of your birth ... with the maiden Mah-Li, if that is your wish."

"I can't. I love you."

"But not enough to grant me release from an odious responsibility," said the Master of Sinanju, lifting his face to meet Remo's streaming eyes.

"I'm sorry, Little Father."

"So be it," said Chiun, rising to his feet like a time-lapse film of a sunflower growing. "I go now to meet my future clients. I will expect you not to interfere."

"What about the investment ceremony?" asked Remo.

"There is no time. I will dispense with it. Consider yourself the new reigning Master of Sinanju."

"I'm not sure I'm ready," Remo said weakly.

"And I am sure you are not," said the Master of Sinanju. "But fate has decreed it otherwise. But you may take comfort in the story of the Master Tipi. I have placed the scroll describing his career under his new emperor beside my throne. It was not so terrible. He, too, was in his end days."

And Chiun went out of the house of his ancestors without a backward glance.

Colonel Viktor Ditko waited in the square of the village of Sinanju, surrounded by a crack team of black-clad Special Military Purposes Unit soldiers. Spetsnaz commandos. A cross between the American Green Berets and the old Nazi Stormtroopers, they were the most vicious soldiers in the entire Soviet Army. And Colonel Ditko was prepared to unleash them.

The word had come from the Kremlin. He was to personally take possession of the Master of Sinanju at sunset, and bring him instantly back to Russia.

When Colonel Ditko saw the crowd of villagers scatter like frightened pigeons, he was surprised to see an elderly Korean being escorted into the square by another. He recognized the younger of the two as the one in the original tape made by Sammy Kee, but not the other, who wobbled as he walked.

Then, with a shock, he realized it was the Master of Sinanju himself. He looked older, shrunken and feeble in his funereal black robes.

"What is this?" demanded Ditko of the Master of Sinanju.

And the Master of Sinanju replied in excellent if haughty Russian.

"*This* is the Master of Sinanju, Soviet dog. What are you?"

"I am Colonel Viktor Ditko. I have come to take you to my country."

"You make it sound simple."

"I understood there would be no resistance," said Ditko, a little nervously.

"And there will be none. But there must be a ceremony. Where is Smith?"

"Here," said Dr. Harold W. Smith, stepping out from behind a group of huts, where he had observed the Russian advance. He carried a very large scroll under one arm, edged in gold and tied with a blue ribbon.

"Who is this?" asked Ditko.

"My former employer," said the Master of Sinanju. "With our contract. He must sign it and you must sign it before I can enter into your service."

"Very well," Colonel Ditko said impatiently. "Give it to me."

Chiun took the scroll, opened it to the very end,

and held it stiffly in the air while Smith signed the bottom. And then the Master of Sinanju turned to Colonel Ditko and offered the document for signing.

"Do you not wish to read it first?" asked Chiun politely.

"No," snapped Ditko. "We have little time."

"Such wisdom from a Russian," said the Master of Sinanju, a faint smile tugging at his parchment lips. "It augurs well for my service in your country."

When the contract was properly signed, the Master of Sinanju made a show of rolling up the document and with a little bow handed it to Colonel Ditko.

"It is done," said the Master of Sinanju. "Your emperor, and you as his representative, are now responsible for all provisions and guarantees described in this contact."

"Of course."

"One provision is that my village is sanctified from harm and that my pupil, the new Master of Sinanju, be allowed to govern in peace."

"If he does not wish to work for us, that is his right as an American," said Colonel Ditko stuffily. "But it is understood he works for no other country."

"For the duration of my services to you," agreed Chiun.

Smith, who understood some Russian, was surprised at the ease with which the transfer of employment took place. There was no haggling over price, none of the last-minute i-dotting and t-crossing that had characterized his dealings with Chiun. But it was clear to Smith that Chiun was a shadow of his former self. He looked so shaky that a stiff breeze might have toppled him.

"Take him to the car," ordered Colonel Ditko, who relished commanding the elite Spetsnaz team. "I will join you at the airport."

"I must say good-bye to my pupil, Remo," Chiun insisted.

"There is no time. The aircraft is waiting," said Colonel Ditko.

Chiun bowed stiffly. "I obey, because I am now in your service."

Two Spetsnaz commandos started to take Chiun by his spindly arms, but he shook them off.

"Unhand me," he snapped. "I am old and frail, but I can still walk. Allow me to leave my village with dignity."

Gathering up the hem of his robes, he strode up the road, the two commandos on either side of him, walking a respectful two paces behind. The Master of Sinanju did not look back. Nor did he say good-bye to Smith or the handful of villagers who had ventured out into the square. Smith wondered if the old man would survive the plane trip. He looked that far gone.

While everyone's eyes were following the slow departure of the Master of Sinanju, Smith slipped away, heading for the beach. It was done. Now there was just one last detail.

Smith found a quiet place among the cold rocks. He dug into the watch pocket of his vest and removed a small case. In it was a coffin-shaped pill. He had carried it ever since that day many years ago when he had assumed his duties as director of CURE. Duties, he knew, which were lifelong, because when they ended they could only end with his death.

"Good-bye, Maude, Vickie. I love you both very much."

And there, on the empty beach so far away from the nation he loved, Dr. Harold W. Smith swallowed the pill.

And choked on it. It caught in his throat. It wouldn't go down.

Smith, frantic that his suicide attempt might fail, plunged into the cold surf and drank a long swallow of salt water to wash down the pill.

The water was so cold, it numbed his taste buds so he couldn't taste salt. But he felt the pill go down. Shivering from his sudden immersion, he threw himself on the fine beach sand and waited for the end to come.

Dimly he heard the percussive stutter of automatic-weapons fire.

There were screams. The haunting screams of the dying.

Faintly he understood that the Russians had betrayed them all. And deep within him, a cold rage swept all thoughts of death—his death—from his mind.

Dr. Harold W. Smith pulled himself to his feet. The poison was supposed to act quickly, but he was still alive. He stumbled up into the rocks. The sporadic fire grew constant.

Smith swore and started running, not sure what he could accomplish in his last moments of life, but determined to inflict a final blow.

He tripped over his automatic, lying in the sand where Remo had thrown it. Smith grabbed it, checked the action. There was no clip, but he had an extra in his pocket. He loaded the gun and pushed on, praying that he had time to take out a few of them before he succumbed. A spreading coldness filled his stomach.

Remo Williams stood among the heaped treasures of Sinanju, his mind stunned at Chiun's strange actions, when he heard the shooting.

"Chiun!" he cried. He pitched out the door.

There was no sign of Chiun. The Russians were going from hut to hut, dragging people out into a huddled mass in the village square. To expedite their work, they fired into the air. Sometimes, not into the air.

A running woman bumped into Remo. He caught her in his arms, then noticed the hole in her chest gushing blood. She gave out a little sigh and died.

A clot of soldiers came around the corner. Their eyes locked with Remo's.

Remo moved on the Russian commandos, his senses coming alive in a way they had never done before. He could see the bullet tracks erupting in his direction, and each individual bullet in each track.

Dodging them was the same as dodging cork guns. He took an inside line, evading the streams of bullets as if they were harmless flashlight beams wielded by nervous children.

To the eyes of the Russians, Remo seemed to float toward them, his feet barely touching the ground—but in actuality he was striking with the nervous speed of a fer-de-lance.

Remo hit the nearest Russian with an openhanded palm. The soldier's rib cage was instantly turned to Jell-O. He collapsed from the sudden lack of skeletal support.

"We have found him!" called another soldier. "The American."

"Right," said Remo, chopping him down like a sapling. "I'm the American."

The Russians broke in all directions, seeking cover in the higher rocks. Remo moved toward the nearest group, pulled them off the rocks like bugs off a wall. He appeared only to tap them, but they did not rise from where they fell.

"American," called Colonel Ditko from the rocks above where Remo stood amid a pile of Soviet corpses.

"What?" Remo shot back.

"We do not wish to slaughter everyone. We only want you."

"I'm not going to Russia," snapped Remo.

"And Russia does not want you. But we will exchange your surrender for the lives of these people."

"You can't get them all," Remo said, trying to bluff. "But I'll get all of you."

"If you wish a war, than so be it," said Ditko, whose orders were to erase all traces of the village of Sinanju and its people. "I will order my men to fire into the crowd."

Remo saw the villagers huddled behind their homes, their faces wearing that soul-shocked look that he had seen a thousand times in Vietnam. He felt a wave of pity for them. They were not—and never had been—masters of their own fate. Centuries of dependence on the Masters of Sinanju had stripped them of all self-reliance. It was not their fault they had turned out the way they had. They were no longer Chiun's people. They were his now.

Remo hesitated, calculating the positions of the Russians. Only a handful remained. Maybe there was time to get to them before they picked their shots.

But then Remo saw Mah-Li being dragged into view by one of the Russians. She struggled.

"Mah-Li!" he said under his breath. She was not wearing her veil. Her delicate face shone with anxiety.

"Okay, you win," said Remo. And he put up his hands.

They came down from the rocks carefully, their Kalishnikov rifles pointed unwaveringly at Remo's head.

"Bring him," ordered Colonel Ditko. "And round up the rest of the villagers. We will execute the American as an example to them."

"This wasn't the deal," said Remo.

"Wrong. This is the deal our leader made with your leader."

"Where's Chiun?"

"On his way to Pyongyang airport. And I must hurry to join him. I am to present him to the General Secretary myself. It will be a great day for me. Now I must leave you."

And Colonel Ditko hurried back to a waiting car and drove off.

His second in command marched Remo to the wall of the nearest hut and stood him up against it. He gave sharp orders and the five remaining commandos lined up in single file, their rifles aimed at Remo's chest.

"No blindfold?" asked Remo.

The soldiers ignored him. They squinted down the sights of their weapons.

"Ready!" ordered the second in command.

Remo saw Mah-Li fall to the ground and cover her face. Her shoulders shook with emotion.

"Aim!"

"If you harm these people after I'm gone," said Remo in a brittle voice, "I'm coming back after you all."

"I do not believe in ghosts," said the second in command.

"Maybe not. But if you don't listen to me, you'll be believing in Shiva the Destroyer."

There was something about the tone of the American's threat. The second in command hesitated. It was a very big mistake.

Before the firing order could be given, five spiteful shots rang out from the high rocks. And, one by one, all five members of the firing squad fell with their skulls shattered.

Remo broke his bonds with a hemp-splitting tug. The second in command never saw the hand that reduced his face to raw meat.

Remo looked up. Smith lay on his stomach, smoke

drifting from the muzzle of his gun. Then he collapsed like a puppet whose strings had been clipped. Smith closed his eyes.

Remo ran to him and saw that he was going into convulsions.

Remo flipped Smith over on his back. The older man's face was turning the color and texture of blue cheese. Poison.

"Dammit, Smitty!" Remo screamed at him. "Did you have to go through with it? Couldn't you have waited?"

Remo tore Smith's jacket, vest, and shirt open with a single exertion. Buttons popped in all directions. Remo placed both his hands on Smith's wrinkled stomach and started to massage the solar-plexus muscles rapidly. He was rewarded by a rapid suffusion of color under his kneading fingers. That meant poison-fighting blood was concentrating where it was most needed.

Remo turned Smith onto his back, so that his head hung over the edge of the outcropping. He stuffed a large stone under Smith's feet to keep the blood flowing to the stomach.

Smith began to gag. He gave a low strangling groan, like a woman giving birth. But life had nothing to do with the sound that Smith made.

It was now or it was all over.

There were nerve clusters at the throat and solar plexus, and Remo took them, one in each hand, and performed a manipulation that a chiropractor would have understood.

Smith started vomiting violently. An ugly black bile erupted from his mouth and nostrils, spraying the sand below. Smith convulsed. His eyes opened, rolled up into his head as if the muscles behind them had lost tension.

Then Dr. Harold W. Smith lay still.

Remo listened. No heartbeat. He felt the carotid artery. No pulse.

"Dammit, Smitty! I need you!" Remo yelled again, and flipped Smith over one last time.

Sinanju techniques had gotten rid of the poison, but not in time. Smith's heart had stopped. Remo laid a fist over Smith's stilled heart and brought the other fist down atop it. Once, twice, three times, until he had established a rhythm. He kept the rhythm going, even though the heart muscle did not respond to it.

"Dammit!" he swore, and punched Smith's stomach to expel clearing air through his windpipe.

Smith took in a reflexive breath. And then Remo felt the beat. Irregular at first, but more regular as Remo kept up the beating of his hand. He pounded his fist in synchronization with Smith's heart, staying with its rhythm, until the rhythms were one. And then Remo picked up the pace, forcing Smith's heart muscle to match it.

When he was sure that Smith's heart would continue beating on its own, Remo stopped.

He waited. One minute. Two. Five.

At length Dr. Harold W. Smith opened his eyes. They looked horrible, like those of a man who had awoken one morning to discover that maniacs had stripped the flesh from his body.

"Remo," he said weakly. "You should have let me die."

"You're welcome," Remo said bitterly. "Never mind that crap. Chiun's gone to Russia. I need your help. I gotta get there. Fast."

"They betrayed us, didn't they?" Smith said dully, sitting up.

"You learn to expect that from certain kinds of people," Remo accused. "Even friends."

Smith said nothing.

"Here's your briefcase," Remo said, throwing the leather valise onto Smith's lap. "Get on the horn and make the arrangements to get me to Moscow."

"I can't. The President has a deal with the Soviets."

"Get me to Moscow or I'll kill you," Remo warned.

"I'm already a dead man," said Smith.

"You sold us out and the Russians betrayed everyone. You owe me, Smitty. But if you won't do it for me, or for Chiun, or for what's left of the organization, then do it for America."

And through the pain, Dr. Harold W. Smith felt a chord being struck. The only one he would respond to.

Smith made an absurd show of straightening out his ruined clothes and opened the briefcase.

"The *Darter* is still lying off the coast," he said emotionlessly. "Their orders were to leave if they didn't hear from me by dawn. I'll call in a landing party. We can get to Kimpo air base in South Korea by midnight at the latest. From there, I think I can still order an Air Force jet into action. The organization may be finished, but I'm not powerless. Yet."

"Do it," said Remo. And forget that 'we' stuff. I'm going. You're staying here."

"Here?"

"You're going to protect Sinanju until I get back."

"It's a suicide mission, Remo. What if you don't come back?"

Remo stood up and gestured to the tiny village below.

"Then it's all yours, Smitty. Don't spend the gold all in one place."

16

Deep into Soviet airspace, General Martin S. Leiber assured Remo Williams that the Air Force's new Stealth Stratofighter was in no immediate danger.

"The Russians never shoot at armed military aircraft," the general said confidently. "They know we might shoot back. Besides, if a Korean airliner can penetrate Soviet defenses while flying at a lousy thirty-thousand feet, we should have no problems loafing along up here in the stratosphere."

"Good," said Remo absently. He was staring out a window. A faint tinge of bluish moonlight edged the wings of the Stratofighter, which had folded back for maximum faster-than-sound velocity once they penetrated the Soviet air-defense net. The soundlessness of their flight was eerie. They were actually flying away from the roar of the Stratofighter's six gargantuan engines, literally leaving it miles behind. Below, lights twinkled here and there. Not many. Russia, for all its size, was not very populous.

"Good," Remo repeated absently, worrying about Chiun. Was he still alive? Had he really left without saying good-bye?

"Of course, we're going to have to drop to about

fifteen-thousand feet and fly slower than sound for the drop."

"That's where it gets hairy for me, right?" said Remo, turning away from the window.

"That's where it gets hairy for everyone, civilian. If Red radar picks us up, they're naturally going to assume we're a strayed civilian airliner. They'll open up. There's nothing the Russians like better than taking potshots at targets that can't shoot back."

"But we can," Remo said.

"Can," said General Leiber. "But won't. Not allowed."

"Why the hell not?" Remo demanded.

"Use your head, man," the general said indignantly. "It would cause an international incident. Might trigger World War III."

"I've got news for you," Remo said. "If you don't drop me in Moscow in one piece, you won't have to worry about World War III. It'll be practically guaranteed. Right now, the Russians have a weapon more dangerous than any nuclear missiles. That's what this freaking mission is all about."

"It is? Well, humph . . . that is . . . The way of it, civilian, is that I can't take the responsibility for causing what we military call a thermonuclear exchange. Even if it's gonna happen anyway."

"Why the hell not?"

"Because if I do, I could lose these silver twinklers on my shoulder. They may not seem like much to you, civilian, but I'm damned proud of them and what they represent," said General Martin S. Leiber righteously, thinking of the ten thousand dollars a year each star meant in retirement benefits.

"You're afraid you'll lose your stars," Remo said slowly, "but not of World War III? Unless you cause it, of course."

"I'm a soldier, man," the general said proudly. "I'm paid to defend my country. But I haven't spent thirty years in the Air Force, man and boy, just to spend my twilight years eating dog food on social security."

"Get me to Moscow," Remo said grimly, "and I'll see that no one ever takes those stars from you."

"Deal," said the general, putting out his hand. He didn't know who this skinny guy was but anyone with the clout to compel the U.S. Air Force to risk a billion dollar experimental aircraft just to get him into Russia had to have a lot of pull.

"You got it," said Remo, shaking it. His ordinarily cruel mouth warped into a pleasant smile.

Over Novgorod, they began their descent. The sound of the engines caught up with the decelerating plane. Remo, parachute strapped to his back, stepped onto the closed doors of the bomb bay. Because it was a night drop, he wore the black two-piece outfit of the night tigers of Sinanju, and rubbed his face black with camouflage paint.

"We can drop you north of Moscow," the general called over the engine roar. "Plenty of good open space there."

"I don't have that kind of time," Remo said. "Put me down in the city."

"The city?" the general shouted. "It's crawling with military police. They'll hang your head on the Kremlin Wall."

"Red Square would be nice," Remo added.

"Red—?" the general choked.

"Remember my promise," Remo reminded him.

"Right," said General Martin S. Leiber, saluting. He went forward into the nose and conferred with the pilot. He returned a minute later.

"You want Red Square, you got Red Square," the general said flatly. "Now, about my stars," he whispered.

Remo stepped up to the general, and with one lightning-fast motion stripped the stars from his shoulders and, with a fist, embossed them permanently to the general's forehead.

The general said, "What?" and frowned. Then he said, "Ouch!" three times very fast as the points of the stars dug into his wrinkling brow.

"Satisfied?" Remo asked politely.

"You drive a hard bargain, civilian. But I gotta admit you deliver. And so will I. Stand by."

Remo waited. The Stratofighter dropped, its retractable stealth wings swinging forward to decrease airspeed.

"Red Square coming up," the general shouted. "You got a weapon, civilian?"

"I am the weapon," Remo said confidently.

The bomb-bay doors split and yawned like a great maw.

"Hang loose, civilian," the general called as, suddenly, Remo fell. He was instantly yanked back by the terrible slipstream. He tumbled, and catching himself, threw his arms and legs out into free-fall position.

Below, the lights of Moscow lay scattered against a black velvet plain. The wind roared in Remo's ears and his clothes flapped and chattered against his body. He squeezed his eyes half-closed against the vicious updraft, oblivious of the biting cold, and concentrated on his breathing.

Breathing was everything in Sinanju. It was the key that unlocked the sun source, and the sun source made a man one with the forces of the universe itself. Remo couldn't afford to pull the ripcord until he knew where he would land. He couldn't afford not to pull it very soon because even the sun source wasn't proof against smashing into solid ground from

four miles up. So he adjusted the rhythms of his
lungs and worked the air currents like a hawk. He
slid off to the right, toward the highest concentra-
tion of lights. Downtown Moscow. Then he stabilized
his fall, his splayed body a great X in the sky, like a
bombsight. Only the bombsight was also the bomb.

When he was sure he was balanced against the
prevailing wind, Remo tugged the parachute ring.

There came a *crack!* above his head, and Remo felt
his body brought up short, like a yo-yo returning to
a hand. The sensation was brief, and then he was
floating down, feet first. The parachute was a huge
black bell above him, nearly invisible against the empty
sky.

Remo looked up. There was no sign of the Stratofighter. Good. They had made it. Now all he had to
do was the same.

Remo had been in Moscow on previous CURE
assignments, and knew the city. He had picked Red
Square for his landing for two reasons: because it
was the largest open space in the heart of Moscow
and because it was extremely well-lit at night. He
couldn't miss the iridescent blue streetlights that trans-
formed the square into a bowl of illumination.

This, of course, meant that once Remo's parachute
fell into that bowl, the dozens of gray-uniformed
militsiya who patrolled the city couldn't miss seeing
him. And they didn't.

"*Cron!*" shouted a militiaman, bringing his AK-.47
to bear on Remo's descending stomach.

Remo remembered that "*cron*" meant "stop," and
tried to remember the Russian word for "how?" but
gave it up when the man opened up with a warning
shot. Other militiamen—Russia's version of police-
men—came running, brandishing automatic rifles and
shouting loudly.

Normally, even a half-dozen armed combatants would be a cinch for Remo to handle, but not while slowly falling from a parachute. He might as well have been an ornament hung on a Christmas tree wearing a sign that read: "SHOOT ME!"

The warning shot snarled past Remo's shoulder. He was about forty feet off the ground. Remo dug into his pockets for the loose change he suddenly remembered was still there and snapped a nickel back at the militiaman.

The Russian went down with a slot in his forehead and a massive exit wound at the back of his skull.

Remo didn't wait for the converging guards to open fire. He flipped pennies, dimes, quarters at every uniform in sight. The coins left his fingers at supersonic speed and wreaked devastating damage on bones, brains, and major organs. Within seconds, the first wave of challengers lay scattered over the gray bricks of Red Square. Pedestrians ran screaming from the area.

Remo wondered what Sister Mary Margaret would have said if she could see him now.

Reinforcements would be arriving soon, Remo knew. He didn't plan to stick around and tangle with them. He tugged on the parachute shroud lines, spilling air, and tried to land inside the Kremlin Wall fronting Red Square. He didn't make it.

Instead, Remo landed atop a long black Zil limousine that had stopped at Spassky Gate, waiting for the red light to turn green, signifying that the car was cleared to enter the Kremlin. The light turned green just as Remo's feet hit the Zil's roof with a dull *thump*. Remo cut himself free of the parachute with short slashes of his Sinanju-hardened fingers and jumped from the car just as the huge parachute spilled over the limousine, covering it like a black shroud.

The chauffeur emerged from behind the wheel shouting and swearing. He got tangled up in the silk chute for his trouble. Militiamen and a few plainclothes KGB agents descended on the enshrouded Zil like angry hornets. They pulled and tore at the billowing fabric, uncovering the car. They almost shot the chauffeur before the owner of the Zil, the Indian ambassador, to Russia, stepped out, demanding to know what the hell was going on. He was ignored while the KGB searched the car thoroughly.

The senior KGB officer couldn't understand it. Who would parachute into Red Square? And for what diabolical reason? More important, who was this incredible hooligan? No one knew. He should have been under the parachute. But he was not. Was he perhaps hiding under the Zil? They looked. He was not hiding under the Zil.

Then the KGB men and the *militsiya* noticed the still-open Spassky Gate and they knew they were all in very serious trouble.

Marshal Josef Steranko had the cushiest duty in all of the Red Army. He was marshall in charge of the defense of Moscow. It was a traditional post, very important in times of war, but since Moscow had not been under military attack since World War II, it was now largely ceremonial. A reward for a grizzled old veteran of the Great Patriotic War.

So it came as something of a shock when, watching television in his apartment in the luxury tower of Moscow's Rossiya Hotel, Marshal Josef Steranko received the first reports of a commando raid on the Russian capital city.

"Are you drunk?" demanded Steranko of the KGB chief, who had called him because he knew nowhere else to turn. For some strange reason, the General

Secretary was ignoring all incoming calls. There were rumors of his assassination.

"No, Comrade Marshal," the KGB chief said. "It is true. They landed in Red Square itself."

"Hold the line," said Steranko. His apartment overlooked Red Square. He went to a window and looked down. He saw scores of *militsiya* running to and fro like ants. Chalk outlines where the dead had fallen showed clearly against darker stains. The Kremlin was ablaze with searchlights and armed soldiers crouched along the top of its red brick walls as if expecting a siege.

"My God," said Steranko huskily. It looked like Leningrad just before it fell. He hurried back to the phone, cursing.

"I want details," Steranko barked into the mouthpiece. "Quickly!"

"Yes, Comrade Marshal," the KGB chief stuttered, and then launched into a frightening litany of atrocities the American Rangers had perpetrated on beautiful Moscow. They had parachuted in, bold as cossacks. From Red Square, the Rangers had melted into the night. Unseen, they had removed Lenin's body from his glass coffin and placed him in a window of the great GUM department store, dressed in female clothes. A detachment of the Americans, perhaps thirty in number, had stacked automobiles one atop the other all along Kalinin Prospekt and then proceeded up the Garden Ring to liberate the animals from Moscow Zoo, stopping to pilfer the American flag from in front of the United States embassy. Everywhere one went, windows had been cut free from sashes as if with mechanical glass cutters and crushed into small piles of gritty powder. The prisoners of Lubyanka Prison had been released and were even now roaming the streets shouting "*Viva*

America!" And the statue of Feliks Dzerzhinsky outside KGB headquarters was now without a head. All
over the city, they had spray-painted an untranslat-
able counterrevolutionary slogan. It was even to be
seen, some said, on the Great Kremlin Palace itself.

"This slogan?" demanded Steranko, who knew English. "What is it?"

"One word, comrade: REMO. We think it must be
an anagram, possibly meaning 'Ruin Everything in
Moscow Overnight.' "

Marshal Josef Steranko could not believe his ears.
None of it made sense.

"These are children's pranks," he said. "Tell me of
the battles. How many dead on each side?"

"Seven died in the first assault on Red Square. All
ours. We have no reports of casualties on either side
beyond this."

"No reports!" yelled Steranko. "Moscow is being
desecrated and no one fights back. Is that what you
are telling me?"

"The Rangers, they are like phantoms," insisted
the KGB chief. "They strike and move on. Every
time we send a security detachment to the scene of
the atrocity, they are gone."

"Confirmed enemy troop sightings," Steranko
barked.

"We estimate anywhere from thirty to—"

"I do not want estimates! Confirmed sightings only!"

"Comrade Marshal we have a confirmed sighting
of but a single commando. It was he who landed in
Red Square and murdered seven brave *militsiya.*"

"One man accounted for seven?" said Steranko,
aghast. "With what weapon did he accomplish this
miracle?"

The KGB chief hesitated. "Ah, this report must be
in error."

"Read it!"

"He was unarmed, by all accounts."

"Then how did the seven die?"

"We do not know. At first, they appeared to be shot, but examinations of the bodies showed only deformed American coins in their wounds."

Josef Steranko's mouth hung open. Was he dreaming? Was this a nightmare from which he would awaken? He hung up on the KGB chief's frightened plea for instructions.

Steranko walked slowly to his window overlooking Red Square. He could hear the sirens in the night, racing blindly from one scene to another, always too late because they were searching for concentrations of troops. Josef Steranko knew there were no concentrations of troops. The Americans would not have dared land troops on Soviet soil without first immobilizing Soviet missile defenses, and this they had not done. Yet something was roaming the streets of Moscow making a juvenile show of force. Something powerful enough to lift automobiles and crush plate glass into powder. Something that could hurl coins with force enough to massacre armed KGB agents as if they were defenseless children recruited from the Young Pioneers.

Something . . . or someone.

But even as the thought ghosted through old Marshal Steranko's mind, he shook his head angrily. It was preposterous. Such a weapon could not exist. And if it did exist, the Americans would not send it to Moscow to stir up such infantile troubles when they had powerful ballistic missiles to throw in a first strike.

Then Marshal Josef Steranko saw the secret weapon with his very own eyes.

It was a man. All in black. Unarmed, except for what appeared to be a long pole. He was inside the very walls of the Kremlin itself, climbing the Ivan the Great Bell Tower, by law the tallest structure permitted in Moscow. The man climbed effortlessly, like a monkey, until he reached the large onion-shaped dome with its crucifix, retained for historical reasons.

At the top of the dome, the man in black plunged the pole into the ornate bulb and shook it once. An American flag unfurled proudly, defiantly. The flag, Steranko realized instantly, that had been liberated from the American embassy.

Josef Steranko stood watching the man for a full five minutes.

"He is waiting," he said under his breath. "He wants something."

Steranko walked to the phone and dialed the officer in charge of Kremlin security.

"Inform the man on the bell tower that Marshal Josef Steranko wishes to speak to him," he said crisply.

Ten minutes later, two green-uniformed KGB officers escorted Remo Williams into Steranko's spacious apartment. The old marshal noticed that the arms of the troops hung limply by their sides, hands empty.

"Your weapons," he demanded. "Where are they?"

"He took them," one trooper said, jerking his head toward Remo.

"And he took away the use of our arms when we protested," the other added.

"It'll wear off in about an hour," Remo said casually.

"Leave us," Steranko said. The KGB men left.

Josef Steranko looked hard at the man before him. There was an unreadable expression on the man's blackened face.

"The penalty for espionage against Mother Russia is execution," he told Remo.

"I wouldn't have written my name over every blank wall in Moscow if I were spying," Remo pointed out.

"Then what?"

"I'm here to get back a friend. Your people have him."

Marshal Josef Steranko sat down on a sofa that, although new, might have been designed around the time Buddy Holly died. He looked at Remo with unwavering eyes and said:

"Speak."

17

Marshal Josef Steranko knew it was treason to escort
the American named Remo into the Grand Kremlin
Palace itself. He also knew that if he did not, this
madman who fought like a tiger would not only kill
him but also bring Moscow down about everyone's
ears until he got what he came for.

And Marshal Joseph Steranko, who had stood at
Leningrad when the Nazis and the Finns were ham-
mering the city with artillery, was charged with the
defense of Moscow and the mother country. And he
was going to do whatever he had to do to safeguard
them both—even if it meant sneaking into the Kremlin an American agent possibly bent on assassinating
the entire Politburo.

Leaders came and went, but Moscow must stand.

Steranko had escorted Remo as far as the main
stairway of the Grand Kremlin Palace. Remo was
wearing a winter greatcoat and fur hat that Steranko
loaned him.

None of the sets of guards they encountered questioned them. They assumed the old marshal was
reporting on the rumored attacks on the city.

"The guards say that the General Secretary is in

conference three floors above with an Oriental such as the one you described to me," said Marshal Steranko, pulling Remo into a marble corridor. "Your friend may be anywhere on that floor. I can go no further."

"You're sure?" Remo demanded, shucking off the greatcoat.

"Absolutely."

And Remo thanked the man by putting him to sleep with a nerve tap, as opposed to killing him.

Remo floated up the damp north stairs. He sensed no electronic warning systems. No traps. Remo wondered if it was because the Kremlin's stone walls did not allow electronic implants—or were the Russians so secure in their capital that they thought they didn't need any?

On the third floor, Remo found himself in a dark paneled corridor with numerous heavy doors on either side. It was strangely deserted. All the doors looked alike and Remo couldn't read the letters on any of them. They reminded him of his old high school back in Newark. Oppressive.

For want of a better approach, Remo walked down the corridor, trying the doors on each side. The first several were empty, but in the third, he came face-to-face with six guards who were just leaving what must have been a break room, if the strong smell of coffee was an indication.

"Sorry," Remo said lightly. "I was looking for the little boys' room."

The guards turned as if on separate pivots geared to a single motor. The nearest one, seeing Remo's strange costume, fired two shots almost without thinking.

But in the split second it took for him to pull the trigger, before the bullets emerged from the barrel, Remo had grabbed the pistol and turned it into the

Russian's stomach, so that the man shot himself as
well as the guard directly behind him.

Both men fell, hitting the parquet floor so close
together that they made a single thud.

Remo was in motion before the two dropped. The
room was small, without much room to maneuver in,
so he moved in on the next nearest guard with a
straight-arm thrust, taking him in the throat. The
man's head snapped back, his neck dislocated. He
died instantly, but Remo wasn't through with him
yet."

Grabbing him by the back of the neck, Remo
backpedaled into the corridor, bringing the body,
still on its feet, with him.

"Hold your fire," the sergeant of the guards yelled,
not realizing what had happened because it happened so blindingly fast. "You'll hit Ilya."

The guards held their fire.

"Come out, come out, wherever you are," Remo
sang from the hallway. He had to avoid a firefight.
If Chiun was anywhere on this floor, he didn't want
him to be hit by a stray bullet.

"He is unarmed," said the sergeant of the guards
softly. "Two of you go out and shoot him dead."

A pair of guards started for the door. The sergeant hung back, his pistol ready.

A head suddenly appeared in the doorway, and
the two guards opened up on it. The head snapped
back out of sight just ahead of the shots.

"What was that?" one asked.

"It looked like Ilya. Ilya, what is wrong?"

The head reappeared in the doorway, and they
could see it was Ilya's all right. They could also see
that Ilya's eyes were open and unblinking, like those
of a Howdy Doody puppet.

"I'm fine," the head seemed to say in a weird,
faraway voice. "Come out and play."

"He's dead!" one of the guards said. "And that crazy man is using him like a toy."

The macabre sight froze the two hardened guards in their tracks. One of them went green.

"Fools!" cried the sergeant of the guards. "What are you frightened of?" And he put two bullets into Ilya's slack-jawed dead face. "There. Now get that hooligan."

Remo dropped Ilya's body across the threshold of the door and waited out of sight.

The snout of a Tokarev pistol showed first, and Remo snaked out a finger to meet it. The barrel snapped off and fell to the floor with a *clank*. The guard stood looking stupidly at his maimed weapon. Then he looked at Remo, who held his right fist with forefinger extended, like a kid pretending that his hand is a gun.

"Mine still works," Remo said casually. The guard fired anyway. The bullet popped out of the gaping breech. Without a barrel to give the slug velocity, it tumbled slowly end over end.

Remo caught it in his palms, held it up for the Russian to see clearly. "Now, for my next trick," Remo announced, and flicked the bullet back.

The guard took it in the forehead with enough force to knock him down.

Remo danced into the room, taking out the fallen guard with a crunching kick to the temple and then went straight for the one person left in the room.

The sergeant of the guards.

The Russian's Tokarev snapped off a series of shots. Remo wove to one side, dodging the first three shots, and then moved to the other, letting the round drill past him.

"You got one shot left, pal," Remo said. "Better make it count."

The sergeant of the guards did. He placed the
pistol to his temple, and before Remo could react,
blew half his face across the room.

"I guess they don't make Russians like they used
to," Remo said.

It had gone so well for Colonel Viktor Ditko.

From the flight from Pyongyang airport to Moscow, and the escorted drive from Sheremetyevo Airport to the Kremlin, the Master of Sinanju had not
spoken a word. He simply stared out the window,
regarding the wing of the Aeroflot jet as if it might,
at any moment, fall off.

Colonel Ditko personally led the Master of Sinanju
through the ornate gilt door of Vladimir Hall in the
Grand Kremlin Palace. The low-vaulted octagonal
room was one the General Secretary preferred for
certain kinds of meetings.

The General Secretary had arisen from behind an
oversize conference table and smiled genially.

"Welcome to our country," the General Secretary
had said to the Master of Sinanju. "I understand you
speak English."

"I also speak Russian," the Master of Sinanju had
said coldly in Russian. "Too bad that you do not."

The General Secretary lost his smile.

"I will speak with the Master of Sinanju in private," he informed Colonel Ditko.

"What about my appointment to the Ninth Directorate?" asked Colonel Ditko nervously, fearing he
would become lost in the Politburo's endless bureau-
cratic machine.

The General Secretary frowned at the raising of a
minor detail at so historic an occasion.

"Very well. Consider yourself so appointed. Your
first assignment is to stand outside this door and see
that I am disturbed by nothing."

"Yes, Comrade General Secretary," said Colonel Ditko, who took his instructions literally.

So when, not long after, the General Secretary's personal secretary tried to get into the office, Colonel Viktor Ditko, barred her way.

"The General Secretary is not to be disturbed."

"But this is a crisis. Moscow is under attack. The Politburo is going into emergency session."

"My orders are clear," said Colonel Ditko, unholstering his sidearm.

The secretary, whose duties did not include staring at the business end of a pistol, ran off. So did subsequent messengers. The phones rang continuously. But there was no one to answer them.

Military and political leaders, unable to reach the General Secretary, automatically assumed he was dead, or fighting off assassins. Rumors of a coup filled the Kremlin itself. Guards, secretaries, and other functionaries quietly evacuated the building.

And so, while Moscow was practically under siege, Colonel Viktor Ditko single-handedly prevented word of the greatest crisis in the city's history from reaching the ears of the one man who was empowered to orchestrate a coherent response.

No one had dared to come near Vladimir Hall for more than an hour when a strange figure padded down the long corridor that led to the gilt door.

Colonel Ditko squinted down the corridor, which was not well-lit. The figure was unconventionally dressed. He wore not a suit, nor a uniform, but something like the pajamas of the decadent West, except they were of black silk. His sandaled feet made no sound when he walked, but he walked with a confidence that told Colonel Ditko that his authority came, not from orders or a uniform, but from something deep within him.

Colonel Ditko thought the man's face was familiar, but the lights in the corridor were widely spaced.

Just when he focused on the man's features, he entered a zone of shadow.

Colonel Ditko brought his pistol to the ready.

"Who would pass?" he demanded.

And then the figure came into a zone of light again, and Colonel Ditko saw the blaze of anger in the man's eyes and he heard the voice reverberate off the walls.

"I am created Shiva, the Destroyer; Death, the shatterer of worlds. The dead night tiger made whole by the Master of Sinanju," the voice intoned. *"Who is this dog meat who challenges me?"*

Too late, Colonel Viktor Ditko recognized the face of the American named Remo. Too late, he brought his Tokarev in line. Too late, he pulled the trigger.

For the American was upon him. Colonel Ditko did not feel the hand that swatted aside the gun, and took his wrist like a vise.

"Where is Chiun?"

"I cannot say," said Colonel Ditko. And then Remo squeezed. His hand turned purple, and the tips of Colonel Ditko's fingers swelled like stepped-on balloons. The tips split, spewing blood.

Colonel Ditko screamed. The scream was a word. And the word was "Inside!"

"Thanks for nothing," said Remo Williams. who collapsed Colonel Ditko's larynx with the heel of his hand.

Remo stepped over the corpse to reach for the door.

The General Secretary of the Soviet Union was trying to call Washington. The operator kept breaking in to tell him there was a crisis. His advisers were frantically attempting to reach him. Would he please accept the incoming calls while there was still a functioning government?

"Never mind!" the General Secretary screamed. "Clear the lines. I must reach Washington!" He clenched the telephone receiver in his hand. The pain was beyond endurance.

Which was strange, because as near as he could tell, the old Korean known as the Master of Sinanju was merely touching the General Secretary's right earlobe with a long fingernail.

Then why did the pain sear his nervous system worse that a million white-hot needles?

Finally, thankfully, the familiar voice of the President of the United States came on the line.

"Tell him that the tapes have been destroyed," the Master of Sinanju hissed in his ear.

"The tapes have been destroyed!" screamed the General Secretary.

"What?" said the President. "You don't have to shout."

"Now tell him that you have broken your contract with the Master of Sinanju."

"I have broken my contract with the Master of Sinanju."

"And that the Master of Sinanju no longer works for anyone, including America."

"The Master of Sinanju no longer works for anyone, including America," the General secretary gasped. Pain caused his vision to darken. He thought he was going to die. It would have been a blessing.

"You are done," said Chiun.

"I am done." said the General Secretary, and hung up. Sweat poured off his brow like water from a faulty playground bubbler.

Remo Williams barged into the office of the General Secretary and stopped dead in his tracks.

"Chiun!" he said.

Chiun was standing over the Russian leader, holding the man down in his seat with a single delicately curved fingernail. The Master of Sinanju no longer looked wan and tired. Life blazed in his hazel eyes. And at Remo's unexpected entrance, surprise.

"Remo," he squeaked. "What are you doing here?"

"I'm here to rescue you."

"I need no rescuing. Who guards the gold of my village?"

"Smith."

"Phtaah!" Chiun spat. "We must hurry home then."

"What about your contract with Russia?"

"This fool Russian did not read the fine print. Sinanju contracts are nontransferable. Clause fifty-six, paragraph four. Since Master Tipi's unfortunate servitude, this has been standard in all Sinanju contracts. Which you would have known had you bothered to read the scroll I left for you."

"You were coming back all along?"

"Of course."

Remo's face wore a puzzled expression.

"I don't understand this."

"What else is new? Here," he said, tossing Remo two mangled blobs of black plastic. "The tapes this Russian used to blackmail Smith."

Remo caught them. "They're no good anymore. But this guy still knows everything," Remo said, indicating the General Secretary.

"He has graciously consented to accept the gift of amnesia, as administered through the kind offices of Sinanju," Chiun said, twisting his fingernail suddenly. The General Secretary jumped in his seat.

"Now all we have to do is get out of Russia alive."

Chiun made a snorting sound. "Passing through borders has never been a problem for Masters of Sinanju. All nations are happy to give us diplomatic immunity."

Remo turned to the Soviet General Secretary.

"You got a problem with that?"

The General Secretary had no problem with it whatsoever. In fact he was more than eager to order his private plane to take them back to Pyongyang—if only the damned People's Phone Lines would clear.

18

The Master of Sinanju and his pupil sat on opposite sides of the airplane during the flight back to Pyongyang, North Korea. Representatives of the government of the Great Leader, Kim Il Sung, were on hand to greet them and arrange a helicopter flight directly to Sinanju.

During the short hop, Remo broke the strained silence.

"You seem to have recovered awfully fast," he said.

"Of course," said Chiun. "I am the Master of Sinanju."

"I thought you said you were dying."

"I never said that. Your American doctors said that. And what do they know?"

"Wait a minute," Remo said accusingly. "You specifically told me that you were dying."

"Never. I merely pointed out that I was in my end days, which I am. I have no more days left to my life than those which lie before me, which are many fewer than the years I have lived before this."

"How many days would that be?" Remo asked suspiciously.

"Who can say? Twenty, perhaps thirty years."

"Years?"

Chiun put on a hurt expression.

"What is the matter? Are you disappointed in that? Are you so looking forward to becoming the reigning Master of Sinanju that you can't wait for me to be put into the cold ground?"

"I thought I *was* the new reigning Master of Sinanju."

Chiun looked shocked. "Without a proper investment ceremony? Are you mad? You know these things must be done correctly."

"I'm confused."

"You were born confused," said Chiun. "Look! There is our village below. And there is Smith waiting for us."

The helicopter touched down in the square, sending up waves of dust. Remo and Chiun emerged and the machine lifted skyward.

Smith trotted up to greet them. He was still clutching his briefcase. His ruined jacket was fastened in front by bone needles.

"Remo. And Master Chiun."

"Hail, Smith," said the Master of Sinanju. "My village is well?"

"Yes, of course."

"It's all over, Smitty," Remo said. "The Russians have backed down."

"They have? That's wonderful. For America."

"And I'm staying here. I'm going to be the next Master of Sinanju."

"Do not get ahead of yourself, Remo," Chiun warned, handing Smith the contract scroll which he had recovered from the Soviet General Secretary with a studied lack of ceremony.

"Master of Sinanju?" Smith said blankly.

"Clause fifty-six, paragraph four," Chiun said. "Should a client ever sell a contract to another emperor, said contract is immediately null and void. Sinanju is not for sale. Only its services are. You may keep this document for future reference, in case an American emperor two or three centuries from now requires our services and needs to know terms."

"I guess you can go home now, Smitty," Remo suggested.

"I'm supposed to be dead," Smith pointed out.

"Now you know how it feels," said Remo.

"You know full well I cannot go home. The Russians may have backed down, but CURE is finished. And so am I."

"Your choice," said Remo.

"I need a favor," said Smith.

"Yeah?"

"I only had one poison pill. Do you think you could—"

"What? You want *me* to kill *you*?"

"Please, Remo. It's my duty."

"Not me. I'm retired, as of today."

Smith, a disappointed expression on his lemony face, turned to the Master of Sinanju.

"Master of Sinanju, I wonder if you could grant a final boon?"

"Yes?" Chiun said brightly.

"I must not live beyond today."

"How unfortunate for you," Chiun said.

"Do you think you could eliminate me? Painlessly?"

The Master of Sinanju frowned. "How much money do you have with you?" he said after some thought.

"Money?" asked Smith, perplexed.

"Yes, of course. You are no longer a client, so you must expect to pay for service."

Smith dug out his wallet and found there an assortment of bills. He counted them.

"I have over six thousand dollars in traveler's checks."

"No checks," said Chiun firmly.

"But these are guaranteed."

Chiun shook his old head stubbornly.

"I also have nearly thirty-seven dollars. American."

"Worse," said Chiun. "You have no gold?"

"No, of course not."

"Silver?"

"Some coins." Smith poured out the contents of his change purse into Chiun's hands.

Chiun examined them. And promptly dropped them to the ground disdainfully. "Not pure silver. No good. Come back when you have gold," said the Master of Sinanju, his hands folded into the sleeves of his robe.

Smith turned back to Remo. "Remo, please."

Just then the phone in Smith's briefcase buzzed.

Smith went ashen.

"What? This can't be. Incoming calls are routed through Folcroft. Those computers are dead."

"Surprise," said Remo.

The phone kept buzzing.

Smith opened the briefcase. Holding it clumsily across one arm, he tapped the keypad. There was no downlink from St. Martin. Those computers were definitely dead. But when he signaled Folcroft, he got an "ACCESS CODE REQUIRED" response. He almost dropped the briefcase in shock.

"Why don't you answer the phone, Smitty?" Remo asked.

Smith did.

"Yes, Mr. President?" he asked hoarsely.

After a pause, he said, "Yes, Mr. President. I understand the Soviets have let us off the hook. The crisis is over, yes. Resume operations? Yes, that is possible. The main computers are still functioning. Somehow," he added under his breath.

"Remo?" Smith suddenly looked up at Remo.

Remo frowned. He made a throat-cutting gesture with his finger.

Smith straightened up. "I'm sorry, Mr. President. Your call came too late. I regret to inform you that Remo Williams is no longer with us. Yes, sir. I took care of that matter personally. Yes, it is regrettable. Very. And I'm afraid our signing Chiun's contract over to the Soviets has broken an important provision. He won't be with us any longer either. My error entirely. I had forgotten that clause. No, I doubt that the Master of Sinanju would consider training another, after what happened to Remo."

Remo watched the first peep of sunlight break over the eastern hills. He whistled a happy tune to himself. It was the theme from *Born Free.*

"Yes, Mr. President," Smith continued, putting a finger to his ear to keep out the sound. "I will return immediately. I'm sure that we can continue operations without them."

Dr. Harold W. Smith hung up the phone and closed his briefcase. He cleared his throat noisily.

"Thanks, Smitty," Remo said simply.

"I can't understand what happened. The erasure codes were foolproof. They *couldn't* fail."

"But they did. It all worked out, so try not to lose any sleep over it."

"Of course. You're right," Smith said.

He put out his hand.

"Are you sure this is what you want?" Smith asked.

Remo shook Smith's hand firmly.

"I wasn't when I first came here. But now I am. Chiun was right. He was right all along. These people are my family. I belong here. There's nothing back in the States for me now."

"What about the background search for your parents? There's no longer any security reason not to pursue it vigorously."

"Funny thing, Smitty. It's not that important anymore. I wanted to know who I was. But now that I know who I am, it doesn't matter."

"I understand," Smith said.

"Tell you what, Smitty. Do the search. But don't call me. I'll call you."

"If you start free-lancing, we could end up on opposite sides, you know," Smith said, releasing Remo's hand.

Remo shook his head. "This village has more gold than most nations. They don't need an assassin. They need an investment counselor. I can handle that."

"I'm relieved to hear that," said Smith. "Then this is it."

"Maybe it's not forever," Remo said. "If something really special comes up, Chiun and I will be there if you need us. Who knows? Maybe someday I'll train somebody to take my place."

"It's hard to say good-bye after all these years," Smith said stiffly.

"I know. But that's the biz, sweetheart." And Remo smiled.

Smith took the shore road to the waiting raft that would take him back to the USS *Darter*. Remo watched him from the rocks, feeling no sadness at all. It was over at last. He was free.

Chiun joined him silently. He no longer wore the black robes of death but a canary-yellow day kimono. Chiun noticed Remo's exposed neck and touched it with his long-nailed fingers.

"I see the blue has faded from your throat," he said.

"Huh? Oh, right. You know, when I was in the

Kremlin looking for you, the voice spoke through me again. But I was still myself. I wonder what that means."

"It means the same thing as the blue fading from your throat," Chiun said.

"Which is?"

"Which is that Shiva's hold on you has weakened. It was as I thought. If you came here and became one with the village, you would be strengthened in your Sinanju-ness and you would be able to overcome the call of Shiva. As usual, I was right. You are Sinanju, Remo."

"Shiva," Remo said slowly. "This whole thing started back in that burning house in Detroit, didn't it?"

"What whole thing?" Chiun asked innocently.

"When I blacked out and became Shiva. I still don't remember any of it, but it shook you. You were afraid Shiva'd snatch me up and I'd run off and leave you without an heir. Wait a minute. . . ."

"Yes?" Chiun said blandly, watching Smith's raft move out to the waiting submarine.

"Did you by any remote chance fake this whole dying-Master routine just to get me back here?" Remo said.

"Stop babbling, Remo. This is a momentous occasion. We are at last free of Mad Harold."

"I'm not so sure I want to be. And stop trying to change the subject. What was it? I know. You thought if you got me here and got me all tied up in this village, somehow that'd keep me here, away from Shiva."

"That is ridiculous," Chiun scoffed. "What happens to you is of very little importance to me."

"Yeah," Remo continued. "You faked it all. Sinanju breathing techniques to lower your heart rate and blood pressure. The rest was just playacting. You

know all about that from the soap operas you always
watch."

"Nonsense," Chiun bristled. "The truth is that you
are so inept and so ugly that the villagers will not
accept you as the next Master. Because of your whiteness, you pale piece of pig's ear, I cannot even die in
peace."

"You're a fraud, Chiun. It was all an act, all designed to get me back here, all designed to make me
so much Sinanju that even Shiva couldn't pull me
away."

"There are worse things," Chiun said. He pointed
toward the shore road. Remo saw Mah-Li and when
she saw him, she began running. Her face, no longer
veiled, radiated joy.

"I think I'm going to marry her," said Remo.
"Dowry or not."

"She is ugly, like you, but she does have a kind
heart," Chiun allowed. "Have I mentioned that since
Smith has broken our contract, his last shipment of
gold is refundable in full? I forgot to mention this to
him earlier and it is too late to return it to him now.
The histories do not cover this situation. I am uncertain what I should do."

"You'll figure out something," Remo said.

Chiun snapped his fingers. "Of course. I do not
wish to throw perfectly good gold into the sea just
because it is not rightfully mine. So I will donate it as
Mah-Li's dowry. But say nothing of this to the other
villagers. They will all want to borrow some and the
treasure of Sinanju is not a bank."

He pointed to the approaching woman. "Go to
her," Chiun said. "As father of the bridegroom, I
must attend to the wedding arrangements."

Remo faced the Master of Sinanju and bowed
deeply.

"You are an unregenerate old fraud who will never die," he said solemnly.

"And you are the next Master of Sinanju in whose hands I will someday place my village and my good name," Chiun replied, bowing so Remo could not see the pleased smile light his wrinkled face.

Then Remo ran down the shore road to embrace his bride-to-be, and a new dawn broke over the black rocks of Sinanju, brighter than any the little village had ever seen before.

(0451)

WHEN THE GOING GETS TOUGH. . . .

☐ **DESTROYER #59: THE ARMS OF KALI by Warren Murphy and Richard Sapir.** Airline travellers were dying all over America—seduced by young women and strangled by silken scarves in their savage hands. Remo Williams, the Destroyer, and his oriental master and mentor, Chiun, must slay the murderesses and save the free world. (132416—$2.95)

☐ **DESTROYER #60: THE END OF THE GAME by Warren Murphy and Richard Sapir.** The game was on—until death turned it off . . . Only Remo and Chiun can stop a video-game ghoul from zapping out the earth. (133986—$2.50)

☐ **DESTROYER #61: LORDS OF THE EARTH by Warren Murphy and Richard Sapir.** Superfly—he's big, he's bad, and he ain't afraid of no DDT. The Lord of the Killer Flies was a buggy millionaire, out to liberate oppressed vermin everywhere. He didn't include people in that category. The Destroyer did. Still, he thought the world was worth saving . . . (135601—$3.50)

☐ **DESTROYER #62: THE SEVENTH STONE by Warren Murphy and Richard Sapir.** A bigger chill than snow. Harder to kick than heroine. The Destroyer was stoned on star lust. Remo was losing it . . . and loving it . . . in the highly-trained arms of Kim Kiley, Hollywood sex specialist . . . and the hottest weapon in the Wo family arsenal. (137566—$2.95)

Prices slightly higher in Canada.

**Buy them at your local
bookstore or use coupon
on next page for ordering.**

∅ SIGNET (0451)

THE BEST IN THE BUSINESS

☐ **DESTROYER #63: THE SKY IS FALLING by Warren Murphy and Richard Sapir.** It was hotter than sex. It packed a bigger punch than the H-bomb. It was a machine that could tap the full energy of the sun. Only Remo and Chiun can stop a sexplosive lady executive from making the ultimate corporate killing—and save the earth from the ultimate sunburn.... (140397—$3.50)

☐ **DESTROYER #64: THE LAST ALCHEMIST by Warren Murphy and Richard Sapir.** A mad scientist has discovered the key to turning base metals into gold. Only Remo and Chiun can stop him from creating a golden age of hell on earth—if they can get past an army of killers... and the magic of a metal that reduces governments to servants and can turn even Remo into its slave.... (142217—$2.95)

☐ **DESTROYER #65: LOST YESTERDAY by Warren Murphy and Richard Sapir.** POWERESSENCE—the cult that is sweeping the nation under the direction of filthy rich ex-science-fiction writer Rubin Dolmo and his sex-tiger wife now has the ultimate brain-washing weapon in its hands. Can Remo and Chiun stop this menace before it turns the President into a gibbering idiot and takes over the world? (143795—$3.50)

☐ **DESTROYER #66: SUE ME by Warren Murphy and Richard Sapir.** India is covered with a cloud of poisonous gases and America's greatest dam is about to burst. Now Remo and Chiun must face the mechanically minded Dastrow who had engineered the world's destruction and who holds the weirdo weapons that makes the world's chances for survival look slim.... (145569—$2.95)

Prices slightly higher in Canada

Buy them at your local bookstore or use this convenient coupon for ordering.

NEW AMERICAN LIBRARY,
P.O. Box 999, Bergenfield, New Jersey 07621

Please send me the books I have checked above. I am enclosing $_____ (please add $1.00 to this order to cover postage and handling). Send check or money order—no cash or C.O.D.'s. Prices and numbers subject to change without notice.

Name _____

Address _____

City_____ State_____ Zip Code_____
Allow 4-6 weeks for delivery.
This offer is subject to withdrawal without notice.